*Dedicated with love to Heath Ledger, my favourite on-screen sheepherder.*

*I would also like to thank Patricia McAughey for all her encouragement and writing tips, and my long suffering family and friends for indulging my obsession with all things Western.*

*Thanks, Lee Van Cleef, for the idea of those burning sheep wagons.*

# Hombre's Vengeance

Fifteen-year old Zachariah Smith has been growing up fast ever since he witnessed the murder of his father at the hands of brutal cattle baron, Dale Bryant. At first, avenging his father's death isn't at the forefront of his mind as he struggles with the harsh reality of surviving alone . . . but then he meets two of Bryant's other victims and he realizes that he must join the fight for justice.

Although Zac knows that lead will fly and he will probably die trying to stop Bryant, he is determined. Zac is back, no longer a wronged boy, but a man. Now is the time for the hombre's vengeance!

# Hombre's Vengeance

Toots J. Johnson

**A Black Horse Western**

ROBERT HALE · LONDON

ISBN 978-0-7090-9070-0

Robert Hale Limited
Clerkenwell House
Clerkenwell Green
London EC1R 0HT

www.halebooks.com

Typeset by
Derek Doyle & Associates, Shaw Heath
Printed and bound in Great Britain by
CPI Antony Rowe, Chippenham and Eastbourne

# CHAPTER ONE

Slowly the brilliant blaze of sunset began to surrender its dramatic colours to twilight. Relieved that the onset of darkness meant reduced work, Zachariah Smith gratefully took his place at the campfire. It hadn't escaped his notice that, being the youngest member of the outfit, he worked the longest and the hardest. When evening time eventually arrived he didn't mind admitting he was mighty glad of it. He'd never imagined that moving 4,000 sheep across country could be so exhausting. Still, despite braving the windswept coldness of a Wyoming morning and spending more time on foot than on horseback, he had no complaints. He had to admit it, he was almost *enjoying* his first sheep drive. Out here the sky and land and seemed to merge together, until the vista was interrupted by the rising magnificence of the mountains. Out here was a world he didn't know, one of raw beauty. Originating from a small eastern town, he had never experienced such dark nights before. Or such silence. Most of all he enjoyed the camaraderie of his new companions – or *compañeros* as Zac reminded himself. Among them was Ed, an ex-cowhand who looked much older than his brief twenty-five years. He spoke less than most and didn't offer up his last name or anything else about himself, But that didn't matter; he seemed personable enough and was good at herding. There was a joke in camp that when he took his hat off he could be spotted a mile away by his shock of blond hair.

Then there was Ramón, a seasoned sheepherder originally from Mexico, who was also the camp cook and prankster. The fourth member of the group was Jeremiah J. Smith – Zac's father.

'You got them woollies bedded down for the night, Zac?' his father asked when he made sure that Zac had made himself comfortable by the fire. Zac looked up, mouth full of some leftover cold canned beans. 'Yes Pa. An' they're in the makeshift corral I put up for 'em earlier.'

Jeremiah seemed to let out a small smile. 'Good *boy*.' he said, with a small flicker of mischief in his eye. Zac stood up and moved away from the light of the fire, feeling a little humiliated in front of the others. He chewed on his lips a little and scratched on the barely existent stubble on his cheek. *Boy!* he thought with indignation, I'm almost fifteen. Almost a man. Ramón come up behind him with a tin cup of coffee, which Zac accepted gratefully. He took a big gulp of the hot liquid but soon regretted it: his mouth was burning with chilli! The shock caused him to spill hot coffee down his coat and all over his boots. When the fire in his mouth died down Zac lunged at the small Mexican. Ramón moved fast, like a cat, but Zac was faster at swinging a punch – which missed.

'You damned diego! Whatya do that for? Huh? Think that's funny? I'm soaked through!' Zac yelled with a mixture of pain and humiliation. There was a brief silence before everyone let out a loud guffaw as Zac shook his wet hands, seething. It was too much to bear. In a blind rage he lunged at Ramón, this time succeeding in knocking him to the ground. Zac hadn't bet on Ramón fighting back, but he rabbit-kicked Zac hard in the guts, propelling him backwards, so that he barely missed the fire. Zac, younger and bigger than Ramón, got back on his feet and this time his swing almost hit Ramón's heavily stubbled chin. A small scuffle ensued. Zac was still frantically swinging at Ramón when Ed came and pulled him away. Zac glowered as he put a sleeve to his bloodied nose and lip. Ramón might be small but he sure knew how to take care of himself.

'C'mon, let's leave 'im alone, boys. Reckon that

joke's made Zachariah a little testy—'

Zac spun round at his father. '*Testy!* Why'd you let 'em do that, Pa?'

The smile had vanished from Jeremiah's lips. 'I don't like name callin', boy. This "diego", as you call him, is the best of men and just about the truest friend we got round here, so don't you go forgetting it.'

The atmosphere suddenly become tense. Jeremiah tried to lighten the tone with his son.

'Zac, don't be mad. We were only funning you.'

A nerve flickered across Zac's clenched cheek as he tried not to react. He shifted from foot to foot, hands on hips, looking at the ground. 'I didn't much enjoy it,' he said at last, in a carefully controlled, flat voice. He was glad of the oncoming darkness so nobody could see how upset he really was.

'Guess I'll go check on them woollies,' he said after an awkward few moments had passed. The others watched him disappear into the near darkness. When he was sure he was out of earshot Ramón turned to Jeremiah '*Perdón, señor,* I did not mean this to happen. I did not wish to offend *joven* Zachito.'

In the orange glow of the firelight a smile played on Jeremiah's lips. He stroked his greying moustache thoughtfully.

'*No se preocupe, compadre,*' he replied warmly. 'Everything offends Zachariah at present, but he's gotta toughen up if he's going to survive out here. He says he wants to run a sheep outfit on his own one day. . . .' The words stopped abruptly as if an urgent thought had just entered his head; his voice became low. He glanced at Ramón and then at Ed before continuing.

'I never said earlier, but I found an anonymous note pinned to the door of my wagon this morning. It accused us of trespassing on private property. I reckon I have a good idea who placed it there, too. Dale Bryant, owner of the Triple X ranch, approached me yesterday warning us off. I told him that as far as the law's concerned we have every right to be here. Ain't none of his business, this is still open range.'

Even though Ramón had encountered confrontations on sheep drives before, his voice betrayed his fear. 'Why didn't you tell us sooner?'

Jeremiah shot him a look that betrayed his own misgivings. 'Well, *compadres*, I'm mentioning it now. No point me giving you the worry to hold all day.' He softened a little. The men were exhausted after a day's work, he knew that. He was pretty darn tuckered out himself. Loath as he was to admit it, he was no longer in the prime of his life. 'I'll take first watch tonight. Reckon he and some cronies might pay us another visit, this time under a coward's favourite conditions: the cover of darkness. . . .' He paused before adding without looking directly at either of them, 'Nobody will think any less of you if you decide to leave – while you still can.'

Ramón snorted through his nose indignantly. '*Nunca*! No!' he added earnestly 'I stay with you. . . .'

'Yeah, reckon I'll hold on too, Mr Smith,' Ed added in his slow drawl. The comfortable feeling of camaraderie hung almost tangibly in the air, and Jeremiah thanked God for it. The rare moment was lost when all three men looked up as they heard, in the distance, the barking of one of their sheepdogs. Already knowing what this heralded, they silently armed themselves. Jeremiah loaded his Winchester, Ramón sheathed a vicious-looking dagger and an ancient-looking Colt and Ed leathered an armoury of weapons that only his large frame could support. Fortunately the full moon was rising, giving some much needed light across the darkness of the vast plains.

Zac had got to his feet when both sheepdogs disappeared into the near blackness on high alert. Zac's heart was thudding so hard he could hear it; he turned his head towards the sound of running footsteps. Zac spun round to face his father as Ramón and Ed came running towards him. Zac thought he heard the grind of hoofs shifting close by, believed he saw figures looming out of the darkness. Suddenly a flash of light caused him to leap back in surprise as a bullet slapped into the ground in front of his feet; another followed, then another. . . . What the hell? it seemed that as soon as he'd lifted one foot he had to raise the other. 'Jeez!' he cried out. His distress was greeted by loud and unfriendly laughter from the intruders.

'Don't reckon you hit any toes, boss, 'cause he ain't screaming blue murder!' came an unfamiliar voice, which paused before adding: 'Reckon you're still a mean shot though!'

The others laughed. Zac let out a shaky breath of relief when his father arrived at his side. Remington cocked at the ready. Ramón held up a lamp and all the sheepherders recoiled when they saw the three mounted armed men, their faces hidden by gunny sacks. Jeremiah boldly stepped forward, although Zac noticed a little fear in his voice.

'Who are you? What do you want?'

The rider of the lightest-coloured mount – possibly a fleabitten grey – laughed. 'It appears your memory is short, *friend.*' A flash of gunshot lit the darkness as the man let off a shot near Jeremiah's foot. Jeremiah remained as still as a statue, the only things that moved were his eyes. He was defiant as he slowly commanded: 'Get down off that horse and we'll settle this proper ways. I won't fight a man who's too cowardly to show his face—'

The blow to his head came swift and hard as one

of the mob sent Jeremiah sprawling on the ground with the butt of his rifle. Only now did the still-mounted ringleader address Jeremiah. 'Don't play high and mighty with us, Smith. You were warned to leave Dead Beeve Creek by sundown today.' He paused. 'We've been watching you all day and it appears to me that you have no intention of doin' so. So I'll say it again, as I'm sure you don't want to be responsible for your men's deaths.' Jeremiah's eyes shot Ramón a glance. 'Apart from trespassing, we oughta string you up for just keeping company with that there damned diego. Messicans are even less welcome in these parts than woollies. Diegos ain't worth jackshit, ain't never no good, thieving as soon as your back's turned—'

'The hell they do!' Zac retorted fiercely, suddenly feeling protective towards his companion and more than a little ashamed that he had referred to Ramón with the same insult earlier. 'This land here is open range . . . and you know it!' Zac yelled. 'You ain't the law!' he added.

Humourless laughter erupted from the men. 'Found your tongue at last, did you, boy? That little jig you just did must've rattled something loose in that little noodle of yours!' the rider of the grey said.

'What noodle? The boy's as dumb as an ox!' the third member of the mob quipped, but immediately fell silent when he heard that the timbre of the ring-

leader's voice had changed. It had become threatening, lingering precisely over every word, a restraint
which the men knew only too well was a prelude to
violence.

'Ain't you figured it out yet, boy? Out here, we *are*
the law!'

The other men had started walking their mounts
close around them in a circle.

The silent attack came quickly but not unexpectedly. With a shaking hand Ramón let off a shot. With
the handicap of poor nightsight he only succeeded
in grazing one of the riders' mounts. A shot was
returned by one of the men, which brought Ramón
crashing to the floor, writhing in agony as his left
shin was shattered. Jeremiah caught a bullet in his
thigh before he could even fire off a defending shot.
Everything happened so rapidly, Zac couldn't react
in time. Before he realized what was happening, his
father and Ramón had been dragged across to the
wheels of the sheep wagon and tied to the thick
spokes. He yelled when he saw their arms wrenched
behind their backs. He desperately ran towards
them, but his way was blocked by the mass of horse-
flesh. The rider wielded a six-shooter in Zac's face.
Although the night had grown cold, Zac still felt tears
of sweat rolling down his back and face. Unarmed,
he stood still, hoping that if he did so, he would
somehow become invisible, and the rider would

15

move away so he could go to his father.

'Obliged for the corral you put up for them wool-lies, kid,' said the masked aggressor. 'It's gonna make my job a hellava lot easier!' As he kicked his mount over to the corral, there was a flash of white in the darkness as one of sheepdogs leapt to defend the flock.

'No!' Zac cried as he saw the unmistakable glint of metal being raised in the man's hand. Zac started reaching for the weapon. 'Don't shoot my dog,' he raved through clenched teeth. 'Don't shoot my dog, Goddamn you!'

Now enraged, the man wrenched control of the firearm back, kicking Zac to the ground. A muffled shot sounded as the dog was hit in the chest at close range.

Zac got to his feet, feeling sick to his stomach when he caught sight of his dog on the ground. He turned to hear the hammer being thumbed back on the trigger once again.

The man whom Zac had heard addressed as Reeve threw two shovels taken from the sheep wagons at Zac and Ed – who was also by now unarmed and defenceless. Zac quickly glanced at his father.

'Well, what you waitin' for?' came the impatient voice of the ringleader. It was unmistakable as he seemed to have a slight lisp to his otherwise menac-ing voice. 'Ain't got all night. Start killin' them maggots before I get real mad.'

When the realization dawned on Zac that the men meant him and Ed to mercilessly butcher the ewes and lambs with a shovel, all remaining thoughts of staying calm to avoid antagonizing the intruders further deserted him.

'We ain't killin' 'em like that after all the trouble we've been through getting them this far! If you want 'em dead why don't you just shoot 'em and get it over with? This way ain't right!'

'No, Zac! Reckon we gotta do what they say,' Ed hissed at Zac. He picked up a shovel and graphically showed his intention to comply.

'Well, it seems the slow farm boy's got an inch of intellect in that thick head after all.'

The man's venom switched back to Zac. 'Now, you little cuss, pick up the damned shovel and do as I told you,' he ordered. Zac glanced over to his father, then to Ramón and finally to Ed, who would not look his way. Hearing his heart hammer in his ears, Zac licked his dry lips before slinging the shovel on the ground. 'Never!' he spat defiantly.

Without warning, the ringleader was upon him so fast it was as if he had flown from the saddle. Zac was pushed through the darkness, a surprised breath escaping his lungs as his back hit the ground. Zac struggled as the bigger, stronger man held him down.

17

'Seems you need a little memento of this night, you little bastard!'

Zac saw a flash of metal glint in the moonlight.

'No boss! Don't!' one man yelled. Ed tried to disarm the masked aggressor, only to be set upon by another.

All Zac remembered was the struggle, that awful struggle. He was pinned by a heavy knee in the chest, crushing him, pushing all the air out of his lungs. Fighting for breath, he double blinked when he saw what looked like a pair of shears being wielded at him. Zac thought the man was going to plunge them into his throat. The last thing Zac was sickenly aware of before the knife cut away the bottoms of his earlobes was the man's huge dry hands, each with a digit missing. Feeling blood pumping down his face, Zac couldn't breathe, let alone cry out. He felt dizzy, as if he was close to passing out. When the mutilation was complete he was allowed to sit up. Zac fell on to his side, hands covering the bloodied remains of his ears.

'Now you're earmarked like one of your precious woollies!' his tormentor said with a snort. This time his two accomplices didn't join in. One of them actually turned his mount away but halted when he heard the unmistakable sound of a hammer being thumbed back.

'Where you goin', Harris?' Zac's tormenter hissed

at his sidekick. Harris looked at his boss before looking down at Zac, who was trying to tear strips from his own shirt to stem the torrent of bleeding.

'You never mentioned anything about you mutilating no one. Dammit, I never agreed to that.'

The boss sneered. 'Since you've such a liking for the boy, you can be the one to dispatch him. He's seen and heard too much. Now finish the job while we finish ours.'

Without a word Harris hauled the bloody Zac to his feet. Zac felt his knees buckle underneath him. He didn't resist when his hands were tied to the saddle horn and he was lead away into the darkness. *Oh Jesus, help me,* he prayed silently. *I don't want to die. . . .*

Suddenly he heard the disturbance over by the sheep wagons. *Pa and Ramón,* Zac thought through his own disorientating pain. The other sheepdog was barking fiercely until a gunshot silenced her forever. Harris paused, also unbelieving of the new developments. The remainder of the flock that hadn't been shot or clubbed to death were being run over the side of the ravine to their deaths on the rocks below. The cries of the animals being sent to their deaths was ghastly to hear.

'God Almighty!' Harris yelled as the two sheep wagons, now alight, were also sent careering off a steep bluff into Dead Beeve Creek below.

'Pa!' Zac cried out, tugging with all his strength against the lariat that held him tight.

Zac turned to Harris, eyes too bright. 'Mister! Please! Let me go to him. . . . My pa! He's inside that wagon!'

# CHAPTER TWO

'Take the Colt, and run, boy! Run!'

Zac stood dumbly for a second as the lariat was untied and he suddenly felt the heaviness of metal in his hands. The momentary pause was broken when Zac heard the other men calling out to Harris. He knew this was his only chance to escape. Harris was letting him go, probably at great risk to himself. Zac hesitated in the darkness for a moment. Harris's voice dropped a decibel to a barely audible whisper. 'I'm sorry boy, but I reckon your pa and the Messican are dead. But you can still get away alive. Run like the devil himself was behind you!'

'Yes sir. . . .' Then he was gone. Zac reached the cover of undergrowth without being seen. The burning wagons below were adding a faint orange glow to the sky. As the other two riders drew closer, Zac put a hand over his mouth to muffle his rapid breathing. By the moonlight he saw the men turning their mounts towards the east, in the direction of the ranch. Zac crouched low, face almost touching the ground. His dark hair was invisible in the gloom. He could see the burning wagons broken by the creek, Zac tried to edge his way down the side of the bluff. In the limited light he reckoned he could do it, if he edged down slowly. Suddenly, a bullet slapped the ground beside him. Zac gasped, lost his footing, half-fell and half-tumbled down the bluff. His descent was only stopped by a protruding root that caught him hard in the stomach. Groaning in pain, he jolted as another bullet screamed over his head, followed by an angry cuss from above. He had to move . . . and fast. He willed his body to relax as much as possible as he allowed himself to reach the thicket at the bottom by rolling and falling.

'Dammit!' came the voice from above. 'You find a way to get down there, Harris, or I'll finish the god-damned job off myself . . . and you with it!'

Zac looked up, straining his eyes to get a glimpse of the men, but the three silhouettes above him were gone. He had been insensible before, but now he noticed piles of dead and dying sheep. 'Jesus. . . .' Zac whispered at the pitiful sight of the suffering animals, knowing he could do nothing to relieve their pain. There wasn't much time. With all the strength he possessed he half-ran, half-limped to the first wagon. It had missed the water, the canvas covering was completely destroyed. He shielded his face with his hand, the heat was so intense.

'Pa?' he cried out, hoping against hope that his father was still alive, even though he knew such a thought was futile. Nothing could survive that blaze. Refusing to abandon his father and Ramón just yet, he waded into the creek where the other wagon lay on its side, half submerged in the water. The blaze had been mostly extinguished, enabling Zac to peer inside. He knew he had to be cautious, for he was aware of the three gunny-sackers following behind him. The first thing to hit him was the smell, the sickening smell of burning human flesh. In the bright moonlight Zac could see two feet protruding from the broken Dutch doors at the rear of the wagon. Zac froze. *No! Please God no!* Then he was gripped by a sense of urgency. His hands were shaking as he pulled the sodden Ramón out. Zac was unbalanced by the sudden weight and they both landed in the water. Zac screamed inwardly when he saw that the bullet had entered the back of Ramón's skull. Now desperate to find his father, praying to God that he wasn't also in the wagon, Zac scrambled up to find his father lying on his side, towards the front of the wagon. He had also been slaughtered in a similar fashion to his dear *compadre*. It all seemed so unreal. Sick to his stomach Zac backed out of the wagon, shivering. Pain seared across the back of his head from the unseen blow. He lost his balance and was met by the cold dark water. Trying to resurface, he was pushed back down and he struggled against the unseen, brutal hands. Zac didn't know where it came from, but an almighty rage replaced the fear and he started to fight back. He remembered the Colt Harris had given him, but it had been lost in his descent down the bluff. Again, his head was forced under the water. With one last surge of adrenalin, Zac managed to turn his head far enough to sink his teeth into the arm. The gunny-sacker let out a bloodcurdling roar. Zac, still gulping for air, broke free. A bullet slapped the water dangerously close by, but missed its mark. The man was going wild. 'Goddamit! Harris! Reeve! Don't let him get away! The little bastard bit me! Took a whole chunk outta my arm!'

Pounding hoofs came crashing through the water and before Zac knew what was happening the one called Reeve stood before him. Zac spun round, looking for the other two. As Reeve lowered his Remington he hissed to Zac: 'I'll let you go this one time.' The words came muffled from under the sack. 'Go to ground, boy. Run!'

Zac didn't need telling twice. Run he did. He ran from Dead Beeve Creek, all the time expecting a bullet in the back, but it never came. By the time he felt safe enough to pause, light was creeping into the sky. Exhausted, he lay down on his back, his ears were still bleeding profusely as he had lost his cloth. Awash with pain, he closed his eyes. *Just for a second* he told himself. . . .

Helen White examined the cut barbed-wire fence with anger. Damned neighbours had been cutting the wire again – it was another form of their relentless bullying. She glanced up as the sound of incessant barking came from behind a clump of trees at the eastern boundary of her homestead. She immediately reached for her weapon, for the dog's bark told her that something was unusual; it was not just a hare or even a coyote alerting the dog. When she got to the dog, she gasped. 'Dear God!' The dog was standing over the body of a bloodied boy. Helen peered closer. He lay on his back, dark, dried blood over his cheeks. Fresh blood still ran from the sides of his face, with the occasional fly landing on the wound.

Suddenly Helen felt nervous. What if it was a trick set up by Dale Bryant of the neighbouring Triple X ranch? Standing back, ready to shoot, first she poked him in the ribs with the muzzle of her Winchester. Although she had half-expected it, she still jumped when the boy opened his eyes.

'Who are you?' Helen snapped. 'What are you doing here?'

The boy slowly rolled on to his side as if in great pain. He flinched as he sat up and saw her weapon pointed at him.

'Begging your pardon, ma'am,' he said, unexpectedly rising to his feet and taking off.

'Hey! Wait!'

He stopped, and turned towards her, all the time suspiciously eyeing her Winchester and his new environment. 'Are the others here?' he asked warily, trying to avoid her gaze. She took a step closer. *Dear God*, she thought. *The boy's scared to death!*

'What others?'

'The men! The men who did this to me!'

She tried to quash her feelings of compassion and reminded herself that this still might be a trap. He seemed eager to talk. 'They came upon us last night. We were moving a flock up to summer grazing. There were three of them, all masked. They murdered my father and a fellow herder before slaughtering the dogs and most of the flock. They destroyed our wagons.' Suddenly the boy paused, as if he had just remembered something. 'There was another herder also. I don't know what happened to him.'

Helen climbed on to her buckboard. 'Come then, we'll go and see. Can you remember where you were?'

'A place called Dead Beeve Creek . . . but you can't

26

go there. It could be dangerous.'

A small smile played on her lips. 'Danger? Living here, I'm used to danger!'

They followed the river until it ran into the creek. As they looked down, they could see that the remains of the wagons were still there, but there was no sign of the bodies.

Ramón was not in the water, and Zac's father who had been left inside the wagon, was gone too. There were some surviving sheep drifting about as well as some still slowly dying from their injuries. There was no sign of Ed. Now convinced that Zac's story was true, a little apprehension came over her.

'What have they done with them?' the distraught Zac cried out.

'One of them must've done the decent thing and buried them. I'm sorry, but we must go back to my farm before anybody sees us here. I am always being watched. And it's better that they all think you're dead also.'

Back in her modest one storey home Helen sat Zac down and cleaned up his bloodied ears. 'Those men are *animals*,' she said when she saw the damage that had been inflicted.

The bottom lobes had been clumsily cut into V shapes. When Zac was all cleaned up and ready for supper Helen brought him out some clean clothes. 'Reckon you're near my late husband's size –

although he wasn't as tall as you.'

She could see he was digesting what she had just said. He paused before asking quietly: 'You're a widow?'

'Yes.' Her voice suddenly became monotone. 'Yes. Ned was murdered on this very farm.' Her matter-of-fact tone was even more shocking than the content of her words.

Zac looked at the floor. 'I'm sorry, ma'am.' He paused awkwardly. 'Did they catch who did it?'

'Call me Helen. No, and for the same reason you will never get justice for who killed your father and companions. I will never leave this land. I promised Ned as he lay dying. You see, I believe it was the Triple X who were responsible. Our only crime was allowing woollies on to our land in cattle country. Our land boasts the extra water supply that comes from Dead Beeve Creek. The Triple X offered to buy this place up so that they could extend their beef operations. But I refused to sell.'

'Can't you inform the sheriff?'

Helen let out a bitter laugh. 'The sheriff is more corrupt than those damned ranchers! Seems justice is only for monied folks.'

Helen couldn't settle. Something wasn't right. As they sat down to a hurriedly cooked meal of meat and potatoes Helen almost jumped out of her skin at the sound of distant barking. It was late into the afternoon, the colour was emptying from the sky. She saw three riders approaching the house from the direction of Dead Beeve Creek. She cussed under her breath.

'Hurry, Zachariah, you must hide!' There was a false floor under a cupboard in her bedroom. Under it was a space big enough to hide a full-grown man.

'No! I won't leave you alone to face three armed men by yourself!'

Her lips pursed in grim resignation. 'Now is not the time to fight them. The time will come, but not today.'

With Zachariah safely hidden, she heard the clatter of hoofs outside in the yard. The table! She suddenly thought . . . the two plates! If they saw those they would know somebody had been here. The sound of a fist on the front door made her heart quicken as she cleared the dirty plates and hid them in the wood pile. Flustered, she smoothed her untidy blonde hair before taking a deep breath and opening the door. She scanned the three familiar figures. One was that of Dale Bryant, with his perpetually red, potato-shaped face, meticulously waxed moustache and expensive attire. He never wore range clothes. *He's a man of substance, remember,* Helen thought with a faint smirk. And he made sure nobody ever forgot that either. His girlish lisp seemed at odds with the aggressive behaviour of a dominant male demanding respect.

His foreman, Chris Harris, stood silently looking at her with his sad, hangdog expression, whilst ranch hand Reeve chewed impatiently on a stick, and picked food out of his teeth. Already tired of their company, she stepped forward.

'Good evening, gentlemen.' She forced out the pleasantry.

'Good evening, Mrs White,' an unsmiling Bryant replied. He stepped forward ahead of Harris and Reeve. She quickly glanced at them before returning her gaze to Bryant.

'We were just wondering if there's been any trouble around here?'

'Trouble? What sort of trouble?'

*The only trouble around here is of your making*, she thought, but remembering what a precarious position she was in, kept up her act.

'We have reason to believe a dangerous fugitive may be holed up hereabouts. You won't mind if we look around. . . ?' Bryant said, pushing past Helen.

'How dare you!' she shouted at his back. Harris and Reeve followed, both looking sheepish. Her heart was starting to race now. Cutting wires on her land was one thing, barging uninvited into her home was quite another. It didn't take the rancher long to walk around the house. Bryant was simmering with rage that he hadn't found any incriminating evidence of the boy's presence.

'Mr Bryant,' Helen said sharply when she saw him heading in the direction of her bedroom. She knew she was on dangerous ground, but she persisted. 'It is inappropriate for me to be in the presence of three men while I am alone, and I will not tolerate any man going into my private sleeping quarters.'

Bryant's attitude changed at once as he remembered he was in the presence of a lady.

'My sincere apologies, Mrs White. I was concerned for your safety, is all. . . .'

'Well, Mr Bryant, as you can see I am alone here. Thank you for your concern, but I am quite all right.' She glanced at the other two men who wouldn't meet her eye. 'What's this fugitive's crime, anyway?'

'Ma'am, I will not recount his heinous crimes in front of a lady. Believe me when I say he is desperate and I reckon he's capable of anything.'

'Then I am very fortunate to have such diligent neighbours as yourselves concerned for my welfare.' For the first time since he'd arrived Bryant smiled, but the other two looked away, still not meeting her eye. 'Has Sheriff Bose in Dead Beeve been notified?'

'Not yet. Thought we might save him a trip.' Before she could ask any more awkward questions Bryant and the others mounted up and left at a fast lope without even saying goodbye.

Helen waited for a good half an hour before going

into the cupboard in her bedroom.

'Apparently, Zachariah Smith, you are a ruthless fugitive,' was her greeting as she helped him clamber out of his hiding place.

'How did you get rid of them?'

'Feeding the lion honey is the only way I know how to survive with these murdering sons of bitches.'

Zac caught sight of an old photograph on the dresser. Without even asking, he knew who it was. 'That's Ned, my husband.' Helen said. 'Only one I've got of him.'

Zac stared at the eyes of the long dead man. There was kindness there underneath the serious brows. Neither mentioned him again as they moved to the next room.

'Something's not right at that widow's house,' growled Bryant. Somehow it had become apparent to Harris that Reeve had let the boy go. They both had shown mercy, and knew that, for doing so, their cards were marked. Neither mentioned it to the other, and definitely not to their boss. But Bryant was no fool; he already knew the boy was still alive. Nobody had ever wandered into his murderous path and lived to bear witness . . . until now. It seemed Bryant was an omnipresent force, an all-seeing eye that missed nothing. What he didn't know he had ways of finding out. Nothing had been mentioned about the kid's escape, and that made the tension even worse. Reeve and Harris passed nervous glance at one another. They both knew the storm clouds of trouble were gathering. They just wondered where lightning was going to strike first.

# CHAPTER THREE

It was still dark when Zac rose and started dressing by lamplight. He jumped when there was a quick rap at the door and Helen appeared. 'Are you leaving so soon, Zachariah?'

He shifted uncomfortably. Only his mother called him Zachariah. 'Afraid I have to, ma'am. I'm putting you in jeopardy by being here. I sure as hell feel awful bad about leaving you here alone with those murderers hereabouts.'

She shook her head. 'Don't worry about me. I'll rent the land to another nice tenant. That way I'll get some company as well as another set of eyes keeping watch.' She paused and said gently, 'I'm very sorry about your father and friends, Zachariah. Where will you go?'

A smile crossed his weary face 'I have no idea. I have no kin anywhere, so I reckon it don't much matter. I just know I've got to get the hell out of Wyoming!' He admired the determination in her eyes.

'Come, I'll give you my best saddle horse. Bayou won't let you down. Savviest horse I ever did meet.'

Zac hesitated. 'But Helen, I won't be able to return it.'

'I know. But I have faith that I will see you again one day.'

After his meagre provisions were loaded into two saddle-bags, Zac nodded kindly at Helen, then kicked the chestnut gelding into a fast lope in the direction opposite to where the Triple X ranch lay. As he settled into the ride his mind became busy reliving the events of the past few days. It was still so unreal. It was as if he hadn't witnessed the pointless slaughter of hundreds of sheep, the brutal death of his father and Ramón. He had looked death straight in the face for the first time in his life. And there was Helen, a woman with more fortitude than he had seen in anyone he'd ever met before. His mutilated ears had started to heal in angry scarlet scars. Zac pulled his hat down to hide them but the damage, the part-missing lobes, was still visible. After a few hours, with the sun now risen directly above him, they came to a shady stream, so he dismounted and led Bayou down to drink and rest for a while. He took a couple of biscuits and gave one to the gelding before taking one for himself. All a sudden he became aware of another rider standing on the edge of the ridge. The sun was behind Zac and it appeared the rider hadn't noticed him in the screen of trees. Zac felt uneasy, and when two other riders joined the lone rider Zac's heart started to race faster. He had only seen the three men by moonlight the other night, but he still recognized them by daylight. One of them was his father's murderer. Zac felt sick, wanting to kill the man where he stood, but he was beginning to realize that he really was still a green-horn amongst these men. Finding this realization as bitter as *mate* tea in his throat, he turned to the chest-nut. 'Time to go, Bayou,' he said, walking him as quietly as he could for fear of the man noticing them.

'Where'dya get the chestnut, boy?' Zac started at the sudden loud voice. He had been right. It *was* Bryant. It sounded horribly familiar. Zac took cover just before lead started flying in his direction. Zac grabbed hold of one of the reins and pulled Bayou towards him. The chestnut was frightened and kept jerking and half-rearing before Zac finally managed to mount up. They crashed through the stream and up the bank.

'Dammit,' said Reeve, 'we can't follow him through there boss. It's too close to the cattle depot. 'Sides, some folk round the railroad might recognize us.'

'You let him go once before, Reeve. I oughta hang you up by your balls and leave you to swing! He's got the widow's horse. Perfect! We can frame him as a horse thief!' The other two made no reply as they mounted up and followed the boy.

Zac saw the trees start to thin out on to open range. He knew there was no way he could outrun the three of them. A bullet tore into the arm of the tree directly above his head. 'Jeez!' His choice was made for him: he put heel to belly and fled. God bless the widow! She had made good her promise of giving him her fastest horse. This land was unknown to him but he saw in the distance what looked like the beginnings of civilization. If only he could make it that far alive. There were hundreds of stock animals grazing by the nearby river in holding-pens, others were visible being loaded on to the cars ready for transportation out East.

As Zac drew closer he saw that there was a rudi-mental town of a handful of single-storey buildings, one of which served as a saloon. Zac glanced over his shoulder at his pursuers, but was relieved when there was no sign of them. Allowing a lathered Bayou a chance to fall back into a slow lope, he purposely kept close to where the noisy and dangerous business of loading cattle was going on. Now Zac saw why sheep were so preferable to these thick-headed beasts. At least woollies didn't purposely lean against you when you got between the railings and them! Through the whirl of steam, human activity and bellows of cattle, Zac thought he caught sight of Bryant framed by the open door on the other side of the track. Zac pushed Bayou quickly to the front of the train.

'Hey you!' a voice boomed out after him. 'What the hell are you doin' up there?'

Zac cautiously looked round and was almost delighted to see one of the hands scowling at him. 'That chestnut should already be on board! Stop fooling around and get it on. Train's just about loaded and ready to go!'

Zac stopped a few feet away and looked at the man dumbly. Irritation crossed the man's expression. 'Well . . . go on and do it, stupid, before boss Wilson catches you!'

'Yes sir.' Zac obeyed, almost shouting for joy at this new turn of events. After attending to his horse, his stomach lurched when he caught sight of Bryant talking to the foreman of the yard. Zac silently thanked God that Bryant's back was turned to him, He tried calmly to make his way to the caboose; his heart started racing when he spotted Harris up ahead peering through the bars of a couple of empty cars.

His luck ran out when Harris spotted him. There was nowhere to hide! Zac desperately squeezed his slim body under the train and scrambled out on the other side. Now what? He had to get on the train: it was the only means of escape. Zac looked up at the car where the frustrated cattle were stomping. He pulled himself up, holding on to the bars and, in a panic, finding nowhere else to hide, he hauled himself into the widest space just above the heads of the cattle, and dropped down into all the wet and filth. The cattle were packed closely together, to prevent any falling, in effect holding each other up.

'Damn. Lost him,' Zac heard Reeve say to Harris as they walked past outside.

'Boss will be mad!' Reeve said. Then they turned away and walked on.

Zac sat in the filth amongst the cattle's hoofs, not daring to breathe. Now that the danger from the men had passed Zac suddenly realized he had swapped one dangerous situation for another. After what seemed like an eternity the car lunged forward. There was nowhere to stand so he stayed sitting on the foul floor, eyes almost streaming from the stench of waste. Occasionally a steer got space to reach its head down to sniff him with a huge wet black nose, killer horns inches from Zac's face. *Jesus Christ, how am I gonna get out of this?* As the train pulled into a station, an unexpected jolt caused one of the steers to lose its footing and crash to the floor. In a desperate attempt to get back up, it thrashed wildly, kicking the others, who kicked it back. Now that the train had stopped, Zac stood up, and looked up at the bars, thinking he could manage to squeeze through before the train went on its way again. When he looked up the hand he'd seen earlier, at the station where he'd boarded, was there.

'What the hell?! What're you doin' in there, boy? Tryin' to get yourself killed?'

Thinking Zac was in there to help the stricken steer, he passed something to him through the bars. 'Here, try and rouse him with this. . . .'

Zac just looked at the goad he'd been handed. What the hell did he know about cattle? He didn't come from a ranch like all these capable fellas. The steer reacted badly when Zac used the goad on it. As it flailed its hoofs around furiously it almost caught Zac on his forearm. 'Dammit!' he cussed at the steer, taking its fury personally. Suddenly Zac's expression changed. He threw the goad aside and walked right up to the frantic beast. He closed a hand around its neck and pulled with all his might, whilst putting a shoulder to the shoulder of the steer. He cursed him as he attempted to will it to his feet. The animal tried but slipped back down again on the wet floor. Unfazed, Zac managed to help the suffering beast. His ignorance of how closely he was dancing with death brought results. Sweat poured down his face as he squeezed backwards out through the bars. He was surprised to see the cowhand still closely watching him. He passed no kind word on Zac's achievement, but Zac reckoned it had been no mean feat. Then a smile came and the other man offered his hand. 'That weren't bad from a newbie. Name's Tom. C'mon, cowboy, reckon you've earned yourself somethin' to eat in the caboose.'

Bryant was silent as they rode back to the Triple X. Harris and Reeve had been riding without daring to so much as let out a whisper when Bryant broke the silence.

'Never mind. He won't get far, I'll wire Sheriff Cottingham in Silver Rock where that train is heading. Tell 'im there is a stolen horse aboard.' A cruel grin crossed his face.

'Now you men ride on to Silver Rock and find that little snake. We can't lose him again! He's a loose cannon, he knows too much. I'm heading over to give some news to a neighbour of ours – widow White.' He paused. 'Reckon soon she'll start seeing things my way at last. And . . .' he chuckled, 'and . . . I always get what I want.' His voice dropped as his flung an acid look to both men. 'You find Zachariah Smith, and you *kill him* this time! No room for error. I've got too much to lose!'

Zac was drinking coffee when the foreman whom he

had seen talking to Bryant earlier walked into the caboose. Startled, Zac looked away. He fixed his attention on the floor, hoping that if he didn't move the foreman might not notice him. Zac relaxed slightly when the man went over to talk with some of the hands. Zac visibly shrank into his seat when the foreman then turned and headed straight over to him. To a seated Zac, the foreman appeared huge, his frame almost as big as the door. He came and sat directly facing Zac. He stared at Zac's mutilated ears for a long time before speaking.

'That horse o' yourn has the brand of the White ranch,' he stated slowly, intently watching Zac's reaction. When no answer appeared to be forthcoming, he continued: 'How'd you come by it?'

Now Zac did look the foreman in the eye. 'Well, sir, Mrs Helen White gifted it to me.'

The foreman shifted his weight and sat back in his chair thoughtfully. 'Expensive gift, son. I wonder what you did to earn it.'

'I ain't no horse-thief if that's what you're saying!' Zac rose to his feet, cheeks flushed red at the insult.

'That's not what old Bryant from the Triple X reckons!' The foreman's grin showed his heavily tobacco-stained teeth as he gestured Zac to sit back down. Zac got frustrated when he looked down at his hands and saw he was actually trembling.

'Calm down, son. I reckon I'm inclined to believe

you over that snake Bryant any day. Your ears are testament to what he has put you through. And you ain't the first woollie it's happened to over the years either.'

Suddenly unexpected emotion caught in Zac's throat. The reality of his desperate situation was only now starting to dawn on him.

'I don't know what went on between you fellas and it's better that I don't know,' the foreman continued 'But I do know he is wiring the sheriff over in Silver Rock as we speak, and Sheriff Cottingham will be there to arrest you when we arrive.'

Fear took hold of Zac. 'But I ain't done nothing!'

'You don't cotton on very quick, do you, son? Bryant pays the wages of most of the law around here. The law is corrupt. I don't want any ill to come to you; we are going to stop the train before it reaches Silver Rock. I will give you one of our unbranded mounts. That should save you a whole heap of suspicion and trouble in the future.'

'Why are you helping me?' Zac asked suspiciously, his brow furrowing. 'Oh, I get it. You want that chestnut for yourself! How'd I know you'll return it to Widow White?'

The foreman only glanced at him and didn't even pass comment on the accusation.

'Never look a gift horse in the mouth, son. Us letting you off before Silver Rock ain't no guarantee of your safety. Bryant and his boys are still gonna be looking for you, if I know Bryant.'

Zac swallowed, then took a gulp of cold coffee to give himself an adrenalin rush for the danger ahead. 'Guess I'd better get ready to cut on outta here.' He stopped in the doorway. 'Oh and Mister—?'

'Wilson.'

'Guess I oughta thank you, sir. Mr Wilson, I'd be obliged if you returned Bayou . . . uh, the chestnut to Mrs White at the White Ranch near Dead Beeve Creek.'

Wilson nodded his answer. 'Will do, son.'

At first Helen White thought the rider on the horizon was Zachariah until the silhouette came closer and revealed that it wasn't. She recoiled when she saw who the unexpected rider was. Dale Bryant. Instinctively she made sure her Winchester was loaded before going out to meet him. As she watched him she wondered how such an almost comical man with his lisp and odd, high voice could instil such fear in people. Maybe not all folk were ignorant of the fact he was a murderer.

'Good afternoon, Mr Bryant,' she said through tight lips. 'What can I do for you today?'

'Well, Mrs White,' he smiled. '*Helen*. I thought you might like to know I have just witnessed one of your finest horses being loaded up on to the cattle train headed for Silver Rock this very morning.'

Cattle train? Helen must have looked dazed, wondering what had possessed Zachariah to do such an unexpected thing. She felt certain of one thing: Bryant must have been behind it.

'You don't seem surprised that your best saddle horse has disappeared,' he said, a hint of accusation in his voice.

'Forgive me, Mr Bryant but I had noticed his stall was empty this morning. It's just I have been unwell today, and not had the strength to realize the seriousness of my loss. . . .'

He took her hand in his, and she noticeably squirmed. 'This lonely life out here must be very difficult for a lady such as yourself. To be without a man to look after you, why it seems almost unnatural. . . .' He kissed her hand, but she pulled it away.

'I do have a man here – my husband! I need no other man!'

Without a word, and much to her relief, Bryant mounted up and left. She watched him as he rode away, her stomach churning, her heart racing. He knows Zachariah was here, she thought hysterically. He knows.

Bryant had been waiting for years to break the widow and now, at last he just might get his chance.

# CHAPTER FOUR

Zachariah Smith stood on the deserted station platform in Athens, Wyoming. Hell! he muttered, immediately regretting leaving the train. It was a one horse town and it looked as though the horse had seen sense and left.

He looked across at the dusty, run-down street. All he saw was some scruffy little buildings of indefinable use. The board announcing the place-name summed it all up for Zac. It was so faded and neglected, it merely read: 'HENS'. For the first time during all the terrible events of the past few days now he realized he was truly alone. Zac felt utterly bereft. He had never experienced such loneliness in all his short life. He wanted to weep and then to scream. Was this all he had to look forward to for the rest of his life? Living amongst strangers, drifting, being no one, *with* no one, with nowhere to go? A ragged-eared freak with no kin, friends or prospects? What would Pa do? he wondered as he stood awhile, not wanting to go down there and face hostility at best, violence at worst.

The more he thought about it, the more he realized he would have to plan and organize his next move carefully, leaving nothing to chance. He reckoned Bryant and his men were probably still on his trail, but he reckoned he'd be far safer in a town. With a small flutter of fear in his gut he pulled on the black's reins to lead it down the hill towards what looked like a two-bit saloon. Zac was pulled backwards as the black refused to budge. In no mood for any more setbacks today, Zac pushed the black by the shoulder until he yielded and allowed himself to be led down the slope. Zac gave the black a bad look.

'No wonder Wilson wanted to swap Bayou for you! Whose side are you on, anyway? C'mon, Snowy! Reckon I need a friend right now.' Zac smiled at his pathetic joke, and Snowy relaxed as the tension left the hand pulling on his reins and so allowed himself to be led.

As they drew closer Zac touched the .45 that sat in its holster, reassuring himself that it was still there. The town looked deserted, the saloon appeared to be closed. Smoke came from the back of the livery stables, so he headed over towards them. He suddenly became aware of his gnawing hunger and he wondered where he might find a eating-house. By the looks of things he reckoned he might be being a little too optimistic.

As he drew closer he saw there were some empty outlying buildings by the back of the livery. He looked at them, then at what little money he possessed. He resigned himself to the fact that the horse had to come first. He wouldn't last very long without him out here. Zac peered into the gloom of the livery stables. He knew it was being used, for he heard the shifting of horses inside their stalls. He called out a 'Howdy', but was greeted by nothing more than silence.

He turned his mount away, then froze when he heard the click of deadly metal behind him.

'What yuh doin', snooping round here, boy?' A sharp little voice came from inside the stables. Zac was a little taken aback, hadn't expected to meet anyone.

'Uh, sorry, mister. I wasn't snooping . . . I was looking for somewhere my horse could get a rub down and a bag. . . .'

A lamp was lit and Zac saw the owner of the little voice. He was an elderly man who reminded Zac of a spider for some reason, perhaps the skinny arms and legs but rounded torso.

'What yuh doin' in Athens? Who yuh with?'

Zac became irritated by the constant stream of

questioning. He allowed a long pause to elapse before answering. 'Truth is mister, I'm alone. Name's Zachariah Smith. I ain't got much *dinero* to be splashing about. Was wondering if you would you let me stay in the livery. Perhaps bed down by one of the stalls?'

The old man suddenly laughed, showing only his gums as the top and bottom teeth were missing. Unsure whether this was a yes or a no, Zac tentatively added: 'I wouldn't expect to stay here for nothin'. Reckon I'd be handy round the place until I make enough dough to move on. . . .'

'Anyone seen you enter Athens? Anyone know you're here?' the old man suddenly asked in little more than a whisper.

'No.' Zac frowned, suspicious. 'Just passing through. Why?'

'No reason. Reckon I do have a job for yuh. You can sleep above the stables, there's a little room up there. Ain't nothin' fancy.' He looked Zac up and down. 'But I don't reckon you're a gentlemanly type. No offence.'

'None taken.' Zac said flatly. 'What sort of work is it?'

'Oh! Nothing too hard. Tendin' to stock mostly. Now come and eat and I'll show you what I want in the morning. Oh and Zachariah, no going into town. Don't want folk snooping around here knowing you

49

are working for me.'

Zac, a little perplexed, nodded his head. 'Whatever you say, mister.' Zac knew in the pit of his stomach that something wasn't right about all this.

From the top of the livery he could see across the cheerless town of Athens. So unlike the town he'd grown up in back East. There were two saloons, both of which seemed sedate. Now that it was late morning, people had appeared. The boardwalks were occupied by people worn down by not enough food and too many hard winters.

He spent the rest of the afternoon watching the comings and goings of the townspeople, any minute expecting to see Bryant or one of his men amongst them.

His new 'boss' gave him a large helping of pork stew before he returned home for the night. 'Hope you like pork,' he said, piling a heap on to his own plate.

Zac's stomach growled at the smell of the steaming pile of meat and vegetables. 'I sure do, mister!'

'Good. You'll be glad of that tomorrow.'

A faint puzzled expression crossed Zac's face before he began to devour the stew.

Later, as he pulled the blankets around him in a real bed above the stables, he told himself that for the first time in months he had a full belly and a comfortable place to stay. He reckoned that maybe his luck was changing. The old man didn't seem so bad, seemed laid back. Hell, thought Zac, I don't even know his name! Zac smiled to himself as he thought one up. Skinnylegs!

Zac woke to a breakfast of bacon and some rough-looking bread. He wished he'd never eaten the bacon when he saw the job Skinnylegs had lined up for him: pig-keeping.

The stench made Zac gasp. Skinnylegs laughed his toothless laugh.

'Today I want to separate the boars out. You will get in there and get 'em.'

Zac climbed over the fence, and he had barely put a foot on the ground when the biggest male made a run at him. 'Jeez!' Zac cried out. The boar ploughed into him and before he knew it he was on his back, looking at the sky. Now that he was down all the other pigs rushed over.

Zac pushed his way up again but the lead boar kept knocking him down again. Now Zac was furious to find himself covered in foul excrement. He hated pigs, with those ridiculous oversized ears and their creepy beady eyes. He hated their teeth far more, though. The boar rushed at him again but this time Zac retaliated and punched him squarely on his dirty, hairy pink cheek. Zac shook his hand where the blow had hurt his knuckles. A little stunned, the boar wandered back to the others. Skinnylegs was fuming.

'You ain't meant to punch the livestock, you idiot boy!'

'I'm sorry, but what was I supposed to do? He ran at me!' Zac saw his boss's expression and didn't need telling twice to get back to work. He started the unpleasant chore of separating the boars from the sows. A light drizzle started to fall. Perfect, Zac thought sourly.

When at last the day ended Zac fed the sows the slop Skinnylegs had prepared. The sight and smell of it made Zac retch. As he poured it into the trough he thought he saw a trotter. Then as the mixture plopped in, Zac saw in it part of a snout, then an eye complete with the lid still attached, the long white eyelashes were still on the half-closed eye. Zac looked away in disgust when the sows all fought to get to the trough first. Cannibals, Zac thought as he walked back to the livery.

He was famished when suppertime came but when he saw it was pork his stomach groaned. Still, he ate it, but this time tried not to taste it. Zac kept thinking of the pigs gorging on other pigs. He figured he'd slip out later, without Skinnylegs seeing him, to go to one of the saloons and see if he could get some grub. He knew Skinnylegs had forbidden him to show his face to the folks in Athens, but what was the worst that could happen? He knew he wasn't really meant to go into a drinking-house, but perhaps someone there could rustle him up something. Skinnylegs had been paying him well, so he reckoned he could afford to eat something other than infernal pig for once in a while! Zac never saw which direction Skinnylegs headed at the end of his first day, so he was careful to wait for darkness on the evening of the third day before he ventured out. Feeling self-conscious about his ears, he made sure his hat was pulled well down over them. He opted for the quieter of the two saloons, The Gem Eagle. Zac pushed through the batwings a little uncertainly and was relieved to see hardly any patrons present.

'Howdy,' Zac said in a low tone, trying to disguise his youth. The barman, a silver-haired man of middling years, smiled, more to himself than to Zac.

'Howdy, young 'un. Hope yuh ain't gonna ask me for a rotgut whiskey!'

Zac was irritated to feel the heat of embarrassment on his cheeks. 'No. Just wondering if there's any grub on the menu. Eating-house's closed.'

'Sure! I'll see what my wife's up to out back. Take a seat, son, and we'll see what there is.'

As the barman headed through to the back, Zac called after him: 'So long as it's not pig!'

When the man returned with a huge steaming pile of potatoes and steak with an egg on top Zac's face lit up. He wolfed it down, alternating gulps of food with gulps of sarsaparilla. He was facing towards the back wall and never noticed a new crowd coming into the bar. He was finishing up his meal and wiping over his mouth when he looked up to see somebody sitting down opposite him.

'Hey,' Zac said, keeping his brown gaze intent on the stranger's grey one.

'Hey,' replied the stranger staring straight back at him.

Zac allowed his gaze to drift off, not wanting any trouble. Besides, this fella looked kinda big . . . fair enough, some of the muscle ran to fat in places, but still big enough to wipe the floor with him, Zac reckoned.

'What yuh doin' in Athens? Just passing through?'

Zac nodded. 'Just passing through.' He stood up. 'Now, if you'll excuse me, mister, reckon it's time to get my horse and get goin'.'

The stranger also stood up. Zac glanced up; the stranger was good five inches taller than he was.

'Where is he?'

'Who?'

'The horse, jackass!' The man laughed, the beads of sweat on his forehead sparkling in the gaslight, even though it wasn't even warm in the bar. He was generally greasy and dirty, and Zac wanted to get away from him as fast as he could.

'He's over at the livery.'

A cloud passed over the man's face. 'Livery? You mean that ramshackle collection of buildings on the east side of town?'

Zac looked around the bar; suddenly it had gone quiet. 'Well, yeah. The owner seems an amiable enough sort—'

'Hey, Johnny! I think we've got another one here!' the man yelled out to the far end of the saloon. A nerve twitched in Zac's cheek as a sense of panic began to overtake him. 'Listen, I don't want no trouble!' As Zac tried to make a break for the door the stranger grabbed hold of his arm in a grip so strong that Zac feared the bone would shatter. In a moment of stress he felled the stranger with a hard blow to his chin. Zac stumbled over the fallen body, but ran straight into another man, who this time managed to get Zac under control with a blow in the guts. Winded, Zac conceded defeat and sat back down on the chair. His heart felt as if it was going to leap out of his chest when he saw the town sheriff push through the batwings. An elderly, thin man with a drooping white moustache and a Southern accent, he sat opposite Zac. 'He got kinda testy when I started askin' him about old man Cousins,' one of the men said. The sheriff held up a hand to signal that he was the one permitted to ask questions around here.

'What's your name, boy?'

'Zachariah Smith, sir.'

'And are you working for old man Cousins?'

Zac paused, until now not knowing Skinnylegs's real name. 'Yes sir, until I make enough dough to move on. . . .' *Jesus Christ, How did he know where I was?* Zac's mind was reeling. *Who else knows I'm here?*

'Does Mr Cousins employ you as a swineherd?' The sheriff noticed Zac's puzzled expression and rephrased the question, as if talking to a small child. 'Do you tend to the pigs?'

'Yes sir. That's why I'm in here eatin' tonight. I'm pig sick of eatin' pig!'

The faces all looked back, all unsmiling. Zac wondered where this was leading. He thought he should be defending Skinnylegs. After all he had given Zac a roof over his head and work.

'Stop chattering over there when I'm talking, Mr Henrys, or I'll ask you to leave!' Sheriff O'Toole snapped over at one of the drunken cowpunchers.

The sheriff, a man of over forty years in the job, recognized Zac for what he was, a misguided, foolish kid. He stood up. 'I don't know why you're here, boy, but by the look of you, I reckon you're in trouble. When I visit Mr Cousins tomorrow, you'd better be gone. He's bad news, boy. All you need to know about it is he likes boys like you. Now, get your horse and get!'

When Zac returned to the livery, Skinnylegs was

already standing outside waiting for him, mad as a rattlesnake. 'Goddamit, Zachariah! I told you not to go into town!'

'I ain't no goddammed prisoner!' Zac yelled back, as Skinnylegs wielded the butt of his Remington at Zac's face, missing by a matter of inches.

'Crazy coot!' Zac shouted as he ran towards the stables, and Snowy. He reckoned he'd worn out his lukewarm welcome in Athens, Wyoming.

Zac was already mounted up and ready to fly by the time Skinnylegs caught up with him.

'Go on, get outta here, you turncoat! You weren't never any good anyways, you *pig puncher*!'

The words hit Zac hard over the thundering of hoofs and the sound of the Remington being repeatedly fired.

'Crazy goddamned coot!' Zac shouted, as he wondered where the hell he was headed to next.

# CHAPTER FIVE

Widow Helen White crouched down at her late husband's grave and tidied away the weeds that she had neglected to clear away a few weeks ago. Since Zachariah had left she had been gnawingly lonesome. Having a man about, albeit a young one, had made her miss Ned more than ever. Although she hated to admit it, she'd secretly hoped Zac would write to her. Then her practical side reminded her that that would be dangerous for both of them. At least work on the farm made her so exhausted it left her little time to dwell on the past when the daylight faded and she lay alone in her bed.

Far off she heard one of the farm dogs barking at a lone horseman heading towards the house. She reached for her Winchester before walking up to greet him. As he came closer she saw he was leading another horse. As they came closer she saw it's coat glisten chestnut in the light. What the. . . ? Who was the rider? He wasn't Zac. . . .

'Howdy!' the man called out as they approached the house. Barking, the house dogs flanked the rider.

'Howdy mister. You lost?' she asked whilst walking towards him, her Winchester held lowered in both hands. The rider dismounted, untied the chestnut from the lead rein and brought him over to the widow.

'Been asked to return your chestnut, ma'am,' he said, removing his beaten up hat politely. 'Name's Pete Wilson.'

Instead of meeting him with gratitude, she lifted the barrel of the shotgun. 'Where did you get him from? Who gave him to you?' she hissed, irritated at how quickly her heart was suddenly pounding. Calmly Wilson hitched the chestnut to the rail. 'A mutual acquaintance, Mrs White.' She started when he addressed her by name. 'A greenhorn by the name of Zachariah Smith. He was most anxious that I returned him to you. As soon as the opportunity arose. I did just that, so here I am!' He wiped the trail grime off his forehead with a red handkerchief and exhaled heavily. 'Been quite a trek from the cattle depot in Silver Rock—'

'Silver Rock?' Helen glanced uncertainly first at the man, then at the two horses. They did appear tuckered out, confirming his story. Her curiosity got the better of her, and she asked him cautiously; 'Where is Zachariah?'

The man shrugged. 'Couldn't answer that, ma'am. I'm one of the foremen of the cattle cars bound for Silver Rock. We let him alight at Athens on one of the company's horses.'

'Why?'

'Let's just say there was some bad 'uns waiting for him to get into Silver Rock.'

Anger flashed in Helen's eyes. 'Them again!' she blurted out. Her voice became quieter, more charged with the emotion she was trying so hard to suppress, 'Do you think he's still alive?'

Wilson looked at her soberly. 'I honestly don't know, ma'am.'

She took the tired horses into the corral and unsaddled them. 'Guess you'd better eat and rest before you head back all the way to Silver Rock,' she said, accepting Wilson's explanation, instinctively feeling comfortable with him.

'Yes ma'am!' Wilson smiled before going to clean himself up.

Reeve and Harris met in the hallway of Dale Bryant's magnificent Triple X home, all ostentatiousness but no style.

'What you doin' here?' Reeve asked, visibly taken aback. They had purposely been keeping their distance from each other ever since they returned empty-handed from the cattle depot at Silver Rock. As the train pulled in they could see that the boy wasn't on it. His chestnut was on board, but *he* had disappeared. Enquiries produced no results, in fact the cowpunchers' reaction was positively hostile. They backed off when threatened with a cattle goad.

Now Harris just shrugged his shoulders, accepting that this moment had been bound to come sooner or later. 'Seeing as the two of us are stood here together outside Mr Bryant's door, I reckon the same as you.'

Reeve looked both ways up and down the long hallway, then lowered his voice. 'Bryant asked me to bring him some proof that the boy we've been hunting down like a dog was really dead!'

Harris lent forward conspiratorially 'Me too! 'cept I ain't got nothin'. What did you bring?'

'Hell! Weren't nothing else I could think of but an old boot!'

'A boot? Was it his?' Harris frowned, incredulous.

Reeve chuckled, showing his snaggle teeth 'Damned if I know! It was just sat in one of them empty cattle cars! 'Sides, as far as I know the boy ain't dead! I heard that from some poor bum who got unlucky at the poker table in Dead Beeve!'

'That's what I've heard too!' Harris leant his weary long body against the wall and smiled a little. 'Well, good luck to the kid, I reckon—'

They both stepped back suddenly from the door as it opened briskly to reveal a smiling Bryant. Both Reeve and Harris tensed. This was going to be bad. Bryant *never* smiled in greeting. He led them into his vast, sunlit office and the welcoming atmosphere vanished when the door closed behind them. They were trapped inside Bryant's ostentatious hell.

'Sit,' Bryant commanded as he took his seat opposite them. 'Reeve, I sent you back to that cattle depot to see if you could pick up that boy's trail. I recently asked you if that damned sheep boy had been' – he paused – 'taken care of.'

Reeve sat rigid, unsure whether he was supposed to reply yet. Bryant leant across the table, picked up the well-worn boot and looked it over. 'I send you out to do a job' – his eyes glistened with rage now – 'and you expect me to accept this piece of garbage as evidence that he's dead? I've had word from the sheriff in Silver Rock. No one fitting that description ever set foot in that goddamned town!' Bryant slung the boot at Reeve, hitting him square in the face. Now Bryant's rage turned on Harris. 'How long have you worked for me, Harris?'

Harris was momentarily lost for words. Then he answered meekly: 'Twelve years, Mr Bryant.'

'Twelve years. You busted your balls and climbed up the tree to become foreman on this ranch.'

'Yes sir,' Harris said, looking straight at the floor.

'I thought you were a man of his word, someone a man could trust. So I'll ask you a simple question now. Did you two dispatch the boy as I ordered you to?'

Harris licked his dried lips and swallowed. 'Yes sir.'

Suddenly Bryant jumped to his feet in a frenzy, turning the table over and swiping at Harris with a china dog that had been sitting on the mahogany table. The dog made contact with Harris's head and broke into three large pieces. Harris fell heavily on the floor, blood oozing through his hair on to the carpet. Before he had time to get up, Bryant's boot was on his throat so hard that Harris choked, his eyes rolling back into his head as if he were going to pass out. 'Liar!' Bryant spat. 'Turns out the boy got on that damned cattle car and got off in Athens! He was seen after causing a to-do in a saloon!' Bryant exerted more pressure on Harris's windpipe. 'Don't forget I'm in charge around here. I got folk watching out for me everywhere. Remember, from now on you can't even take a crap without me knowing about it!'

Seeing his suffering friend on the floor, Reeve at last plucked up some courage to face Bryant. 'The boy is long gone, sir. He won't be back.'

As if a shadow had passed from his face, Bryant slowly started looking almost sane. He lifted his boot off Harris's throat, leaving him coughing and gasping on the floor. Bryant looked at him with disgust.

63

'Well, Mr Harris, reckon you've lost your foreman's job. I'll give it to a younger, smarter man, a man I can trust. You two will still work at the Triple X, though. But now you'll be mending fences, castrating calves, all those low, menial jobs no other sonofabitch wants to do. And don't even think about tryin' to leave here. You've seen what I can do. I'm building a reputation in Dead Beeve Creek; ain't no one gonna ruin it! Especially not a pair of no-good ranch stiffs like you—'

All three looked up at the light knock on the door. Before Bryant answered, his ten-year-old daughter had already entered the room. She was a pretty, brown-haired girl with teeth a little too large for her mouth, a little like her father's. Harris and Reeve had never seen him flinch at being caught out by anyone before. Sheepishly he started tidying up the room.

'What happened in here, Daddy?' she asked, looking around the room.

'Nothing, Livvy-Jo. Nothing you need worry about. We were just moving a few things around in here.' He looked over at Reeve and Harris. 'Weren't we, boys?'

'Uh, yes ma'am . . . miss,' replied Harris, whilst a brooding Reeve said nothing. Bryant turned to his daughter. 'Thought I told you not to come in here when I have company, young lady.'

Livvy-Jo pursed her lips. 'I didn't know you *had*

company, Daddy! You said we were going into Beeve Creek this morning to buy me that new dress I saw. You promised!'

Bryant rubbed his forehead as he suddenly remembered. She would be going back East, to that expensive school for young ladies, and he had promised her a new dress.

'Come along then, Livvy. A promise is a promise, after all. . . .' When the girl was out of earshot he turned and threw the two men a dark look. 'Report to me in the morning, you no-good goddamned' – he searched for a word – '*peons*!'

Both Reeve and Harris took the long way back to the bunkhouse, each of them lighting a smoke with unsteady hands. After a long silence, Reeve blew out his pent-up anger in a long cloud of smoke.

'Ain't right what he's doin' to us, friend,' he said without looking at Harris. 'I ain't busted my balls on this ranch for all these years to be treated like this; it ain't right.'

Harris nodded slowly in agreement. 'Reckon you're right, but I'm just plain glad I ain't leavin' the Triple X in a wooden jacket!'

'That li'l girl of his seems the only thing in the world to make him almost turn into a human being. Wonder what he'd do if anything happened to that sweet li'l thing. . . ?'

Harris looked at Reeve with alarm. 'Now hold on a

minute, Reeve, leave that little girl outta this. She's ain't done nothin' to us. 'Sides, what d'ya think you'd achieve? Law's on Bryant's side in whatever he says or does.'

Reeve shrugged his shoulders. 'Aw, calm down, you old lady. I was gonna hide her in someplace for a few days and watch old Bryant sweat it out!'

Harris walked quickly away from Reeve towards the bunkhouse. 'I ain't hearing this, Reeve. Her ma's dead and she's got a plumb crazy killer for a father. She don't deserve getting dragged into any of this. And when Bryant finds out . . . I ain't going to hell with you!'

# CHAPTER SIX

Zachariah Smith was no more. Like a snake shedding its former self, Zac had been forced by circumstances to do the same. 'Zachariah' had been green, naïve and an innocent. A boy. Now he was fast becoming somebody he didn't even like.

Zac sometimes thought with a wry smile of the first pseudonym he'd tried. 'John Gaymers' had been short lived, due to the fact that he forgot to answer when people addressed him by it. The next choice made a little more sense, as it was closer to his own name. He was now being known as 'Jedediah Johnson'. It sounded similar to his father's name, Jeremiah, so he felt comfortable with that. The further he drifted from Wyoming, the easier he found it to forget about that terrible night. Even the frequent flashbacks and nightmares seemed to decrease after the first year or so. Hard toil seemed to help him into an oblivious slumber every night. He had managed to live through the mental and physical anguish of having no food or shelter, the spells of not eating for days at a time, sleeping out in wet clothes. His closest friend now was the liquor bottle. It was the friend that kept him going, no questions asked.

Now he was returning from the longest goddamned cattle drive he'd ever been on. The crew and their mounts became restless when town came into view. With an almighty roar, the jubilant cowboys rode into Balder's End, in a whoop of loud cheers and a cloud of dust. Zac was the was the only cowboy not to enter town at a gallop. Instead he followed on, helped bed the cattle down, then picked up his wages from his boss. He blew a long sigh of relief as he walked through the dirt. His horse was over in the livery, so now Zac wanted to find a bathhouse, an eating-house, then a saloon. And in that order. Most cowboys had descended upon the cowtown looking to lose their money rather more quickly than they'd earned it, with alcohol, poker and women. Zac was only interested in the alcohol.

He glanced at his new surroundings with little interest. All these end-of-trail towns seemed the same – dirty, noisy and hot. In the barber's shop the cook from the drive was getting a haircut and shave. Some other cowboys were checking out the new shirts in the clothing store. Zac suddenly forgot about getting a bath, or some chow and decided he needed a drink more.

The Golden Bull saloon was already full up with the men from the drive; some were already drunk and getting into fisticuffs. Aggravated by the discordant piano music and loud voices, Zac found a quieter place in the other lounge, where he pulled up a stool and downed a shot of whiskey before starting on his beer. A stranger came and stood uncomfortably close to him, staring at his face, observing the hair then looking back to his face again. Zac slipped off the bar stool and stood up straight.

'Something I can do for you, friend?' he asked, wiping beer foam from the weedy little youthful beard he was intent on growing.

Now that he had a chance to stare back at the man he was unnerved, for somehow the stranger wasn't quite unfamiliar to him. He was used to men wanting to fight him because of his appearance, but this was different.

'Don't mean no harm, mister, it's just you look like an acquaintance I met back on the cattle railway a few years back.'

Zac caught his breath. The stranger saw the reaction in Zac's eyes and Zac knew he must stop this before it went any further. 'You must be mistaken, mister,' he growled in a low voice.

'No, no, you went in that damned car with all those loco steers, and then we let you out in Athens, Wyoming—' Zac grabbed a fistful of shirt collar and frogmarched the stranger to the batwings, anything to silence his blabbering mouth.

'You ain't seen nothin'.' Zac threatened. 'Reckon you mistaken me for someone else, mister.'

The older man laughed. 'Almost had me fooled! Growing your hair long over those ragged ears of yours was a good idea! And the little beard! Hell, the last few years ain't been kind to you, I reckon. You look just about worn out. That hair disguises you, but there's one thing you can't change: those damned dark brooding eyes of yours.' The punch came hard and unexpected. *Dammit*, Zac cursed as he shook his knuckles at the pain. It had been a hard punch, but it didn't keep the stranger disabled for long.

'Now, that ain't friendly!' the man said through bloodied lips, swinging hard at Zac's chin. Zac was faster than the older man, who he still succeeded in catching him on the cheekbone.

Zac blocked the next punch. Now there were other hands upon them, clawing and pulling them by their clothes as though they were little more than rag dolls.

'It says it above the bar! Can't you bums read?' the hard-looking landlady shouted above the din. 'No guns, no fighting! Anything bothering you, you take it out on to the goddamned street!'

The next thing Zac knew he was connecting hard with the boardwalk. The stranger landed a few feet away. A little dazed, they sat blinking at one another for a few moments.

The stranger was first to his feet and he came towards Zac, who in turn drew his Colt, thumb clicking back the hammer slowly.

'Don't come any closer,' he snarled. 'What do you want with me?' He paused. 'That was years ago. Let me be!' Then suddenly, as if somebody had lifted a gauze veil in front of his eyes, he double-blinked as if for the first time he saw clearly. '*Tom?* You're Tom? From the stock cars in Dead Beeve Creek?'

That deep amiable laugh came again. 'Listen, I know those men were after you. Whatever they accused you of and whether you're guilty or not I don't much care. I left that thankless job on the stock cars years ago when I moved back to Balder's End. My daddy died and someone had to help Ma at his little ranch. Was just passing time of day with you, is all. Still, it's odd we've seen each other again. Small world, I reckon. Glad to see you're still alive!'

'Yeah,' Zac said, not taking his eyes off Tom for a second, but he did leather his Colt.

'Let me buy you a drink across the way, Zachariah, seeing's as we're not welcome in that piss-hole of a place. Good riddance, I say!'

Over the road, Tom bought two whiskeys and placed them both in front of Zac. 'Got a proposition for you, Zac. I told you about Ma's ranch. Reckon we could do with a fella like you around the place.'

Zac sat there motionless. Secretly he rejoiced, wanted to accept the unexpected offer straight away. At last, no more damned hard graft for little reward, perhaps a chance of some kind of security, routine. He didn't dare to even think of it: a sense of belonging amongst people he could learn to trust after all these years. Zac's thoughts must have wandered for longer than he realized, for he became aware of Tom's slightly impatient fingers drumming on the table. 'Well, cowboy, what do you say?'

Zac shook his head. 'You can get yourself another cowboy easy enough; doesn't have to be me—'

'No! After what I saw you do that day in the car with those bullocks, I want a man like you on my team!'

For the first time in what seemed like years, Zac smiled. A real smile, one that lifted his cheeks up high, unlike his sometimes sardonic one. 'Well, I must admit it sounds an attractive proposition, Tom. That last cattle drive was hell on earth, stampedes, sickness. God awful food! I always tell myself when I finish, never again! Until I run out of *dinero* again. . . .'

Tom nodded thoughtfully. 'I can imagine. Never done a trail drive myself but a lot of folks I've spoken to say once is enough, and never again.'

'As if most of us bums have got the choice to quit. . . .' Zac muttered to himself. He suddenly willed himself out of the pleasant conversation. He told himself he must remain vigilant. Why should he trust Tom? After all, he had the upper hand in knowing about Zac's past and the men who wanted Zac dead. But he knew nothing about Tom; they'd only met once briefly. Zac gave Tom a sidelong glance. He reckoned that if need be, he could beat him in a fight. That little bout of fisticuffs just then had confirmed he could have licked him. Over the years Zac had trained himself to be a deadly shot. Zac didn't know why, but without thinking he asked: 'Didn't my appearance fool you, then?'

All of a sudden he became the uncertain fifteen-year-old boy of a few years ago. He didn't wait for the answer but continued: 'If I come with you, you must never tell anyone about who I am . . . or was. I reckon a lazy tongue wagging's gonna get me killed.'

Zac paused, eyes suddenly too bright. 'I want that time erased from my memory for ever.'

'You have my word, Zachariah,' Tom pledged solemnly.

'Who's Zachariah? Name's Jedediah Johnson,' Zac said, unsmiling.

A smile crossed Tom's lips. 'Whatever you say, *Jedediah.*'

As they set off for the ranch the next morning Tom wondered what exactly had happened to Zachariah. He was a still a young man, but was looking almost twice his age with the unkempt hair and beard, thin face and even thinner frame.

Tom didn't know for sure, but had heard tales from foreman Wilson that Zac's injuries were the scars of a range war fracas. Tom had also heard talk that Dale Bryant, owner of the Triple X, had been behind the attack, and the murders of Zachariah's father and their Mexican employee. But that couldn't be proved, as no bodies had been found, no authorities notified. No witnesses. Tom glanced at Zac. *No witnesses?* He was burning to know the truth, but decided to ask no questions.

Zac settled quickly into ranch life. The days turned into months, the months into years, and never once did Zac speak about his past. And never once did Tom or anyone on the ranch ask him about it, and the whole arrangement suited everyone just fine.

Little did Zac, or anyone else on the ranch, realize that Zac's tranquil ranch days were about to come to an end.

# CHAPTER SEVEN

Zachariah Smith let out a long but satisfied sigh as he wiped an arm across his damp forehead. That was the last of the mustangs herded into the corral. Damned hard work, but it was worth it, and he was happy. He'd already told Tom which were the one or two animals he thought he'd like to take on for himself. Some others they'd sell to the army, the rest locally. The money they made from the sale of the mustangs sure helped finance the small ranch.

Zac grinned as he saw Tom approaching him. 'All in, boss!'

Tom slapped a gloved hand on Zac's shoulder. 'Reckon we did good today, Jedediah.'

Tom's voice was distant, as if his mind was on other matters. After all their five years together, Zac knew when something was eating Tom.

'Something botherin' you, Tom?'

Tom turned to face Zac. 'I reckon so, Jed. Ma said when we were out a boy was sniffing around the place, asking if we knew the whereabouts of a certain Zachariah Smith.'

It was as if a fist had been punched into Zac's belly, he reacted as if he'd been physically attacked.

When he looked up, his face was ashen. 'Did she know who he was?' Zac paused and lowered his voice. 'Was it Bryant? Or one of his men?'

Tom shook his head. 'No, reckon not. Ma reckons he's from the real south of here, not a white man. A Mexican.'

Zac's heart quickened. 'A Mexican?' he repeated. Zac lapsed into deep thought until a curious Tom couldn't bear the suspense any longer.

'So, Jed, you reckon you know him?'

*Not unless old Ramón's come back from the dead*, thought Zac, feeling bitter to be reminded of all that he had tried so hard to forget. Ramón was the only Mexican he had ever known.

'No. Can't see how, but it's going a way back if he's asking for me by my real name. . . .'

Tom shrugged. 'Well, Ma reckons he's gone. He wouldn't be welcome here; she's never had much time for diegos. . . .'

Zac rolled his eyes. 'Mrs Meyers never had much time for me when I first turned up here either. Hardly said a word to me in the first year.'

76

'And you weren't exactly a man of many words yourself, Jed! Were times when stringing two sentences together was too much like hard work for you!'

Zac held his hands up, grinning. '*Touché!*'

Despite the banter, Zac remained a little shaken. Still, his stomach was master of all and was dictating that he finish up his chores quickly before supper. As he finished tending to his saddle horse in the stables, he thought he saw a quick movement in his peripheral vision. Rubbing his eyes, Zac reckoned he was more tuckered out than he'd realized.

'*Buenas tardes*, Señor Smith!'

Zac spun around at the voice, instantly cursing himself for responding. He barked aggressively: 'Ain't no Smith here *señor.*'

The stranger strolled towards Zac, ribbing him in Spanish. Zac's jaw clenched tight. 'Don't talk that mumbo jumbo to me, boy! If I can help it, I don't speak all that gibberish!'

The young man was now standing directly in front of him and gave a quick laugh.

'I know, *Zachito*! My father told us!'

Zac rushed at him; he just wanted to make all the talk stop! *My God*! his mind screamed, *who is he, who is he?* The man was shorter and lighter than Zac, who almost lifted him off the floor when he rammed him up against the beam. Zac grabbed a fistful of the

77

stranger's collar and aimed his unleathered Colt at him. With lightning reflexes, the man got time to push Zac's wave of thick chestnut brown hair aside, revealing the mutilated ears beneath. His reaction was as if he had struck gold. He caught his breath, then started to shout: '*A Dios muchas gracias*! It is *him*!' He looked at Zac with tears in his eyes. 'You *are* Zachariah Smith!'

Zac's eyes flashed with rage at the humiliation of somebody seeing his ears. He tightened his hold on the man's neck, his voice now became a dangerous hiss.

'Whoever you are, I ain't Zachariah Smith, I'm Jedediah Johnson. What do you want? Who sent you?'

'He giving you trouble, Jedediah?' Tom's voice came from the doorway. He entered the gloom cautiously, his pistol covering the young man.

'Nothing I can't handle, Tom.'

Without warning Tom grabbed the young stranger out of Zac's hold and punched him hard in the face. The man fell backwards, covered in blood from his smashed nose. Zac looked at Tom, open-mouthed. He had never seen him display such aggression to anyone before, not even a farm dog. Tom hadn't finished with the stranger. He swung a boot at his guts, but missed when the boy rolled aside with lightning reflexes.

'Who sent you?' Tom yelled. 'That bastard Bryant? Answer me!'

The boy held a shirtsleeve to his nose to stanch the flow of blood from his nose. Zac had seen enough, and stood between Tom and the boy. '*Está bien,*' Zac reassured the boy, motioning for Tom to back away.

'What's going on here, Jed?' Tom was confused that Zac had spoken to the boy in his own language. Zac gave the boy a strip of cloth to hold to stem the bleeding from his nose.

'I don't know, Tom. But I reckon I want to know who he is and what he's doin' here.'

There was a long silence as Tom looked from Zac to the boy and back again.

'Be careful, Jed. It's unlike you to trust anyone. Maybe Bryant's got a price on your head. I know it seems unlikely, but maybe this scrawny rat is a bounty hunter.' Tom turned back towards the house, irritably slapping his gloves against his thigh. 'You ain't in for supper in an hour, I'll send out a search party!' he hollered over his shoulder, only half-joking.

Zac and the scruffy boy watched Tom leave the stables. Then Zac gasped as he felt the cold metal on his throat. The boy had pulled a concealed blade on him.

'Could've killed you, *amigo*!' he whispered, chuckling as he withdrew it.

'Sonofabitch! You're quick!' Zac cursed, tentatively touching his throat, expecting to find blood there. Although he hated to admit it, he had to admire the boy's skill. He sighed.

'Reckon it's time we introduced ourselves, diego! You'd better tell me why you're here, boy. Mrs Meyers the owner, don't much like your type. . . .'

'*No más diego! No me gusto! Yo no soy sin nombre, Señor Smith!*' He grinned. '*I am Nestor. Nestor Hernandez. Son of Ramón Hernandez.*'

Zac started as if the name was a blow. '*R-Ramón?*' he stuttered.

'*Sí.*' Now the grin had vanished and Nestor's brow knotted. 'I am here to take you back to Dead Beeve Creek.'

Zac sprang back, clawing for his Colt. 'Damn you!' he cried, firing a shot that narrowly missed Nestor's left foot. Nestor looked at the floor calmly, then walked towards Zac. Zac pointed at Nestor's forehead. 'Don't come any closer!'

'I made this journey to ask for your help. Seems there's no one else who can do it, not even me. You are the only victim ever to survive attempted murder at Bryant's hands, the only one strong enough to stand up to him. Señora Helen White is in trouble. She asked me to find you, she never gave up hope that you were still alive.'

Zac lowered the weapon slightly. 'Helen?' Then anger overtook him 'How in the hell do you know

Mrs White?'

'I run sheep on her land!'

'Liar.' Zac raised the Colt again. 'If that's true, how did you stand up to that murderous bastard Bryant?'

Zac watched the young man's reaction carefully. Nestor looked earnest.

'There are a few of us, *señor*. I came to get close enough to kill the bastard that murdered my father. But it was harder to get close to Bryant than I thought. He has become the most important man in Dead Beeve Creek. He now owns most of the stores and is running for mayor in three weeks' time! Now we stay to protect the *señora*. And wait for the day I might avenge my dear father. Things have changed for the worse, in seven years. Anyone opposing Bryant or his men, just . . . disappears, his body is never found. Señor Bryant now openly forces himself on Señora White. His workers have started poisoning our water supply, openly killing the sheep! The local law will not help her – a widow with all Mexican herders, working *sheep*! No one would help her, for fear of retribution.'

Zac listened to this speech with close attention, then shrugged his shoulders in a show of mock uninterest. 'Well, what you want me to do about it, Nestor? Ain't none of my business any more—'

Zac was taken off guard when Nestor slammed him up against the wall. 'You hide out here, like *you* were the criminal!' In his anger Nestor started to stumble over his English. 'It's up to you to stop Bryant! The *señora* has treated you like a son, as she does me. I *owe* her, Señor Smith.' He paused. 'And so do you. She saved your scrawny ass!'

Zac made for the door, sweat pouring down his face. 'I ain't goin' back to that place! You hear me!' His voice cracked as he started to yell: 'I ain't goin' back! It was there I watched my father *burn*!'

'*Sí*! And mine died right along with him!' Nestor spat back. The two men stood facing each other, both tormented by their own grief. As their breathing slowly returned to normal Nestor was the first to soften his fierce expression.

'I was only eight years old when it happened, *amigo*. I've waited the past seven years to seek vengeance for him. I am his only son, all the other *niñas* are girls. I drew the short straw, no?'

Zac had turned away, yet Nestor continued speaking. 'You can keep running to the end of the world, *amigo*, but you can never escape memory. Your father was a great man. Are you an *hombre* at last, *compadre*? Or still a *chavito*?'

Nestor placed a small, dog-eared photograph in Zac's hand. 'This is proof that I am who I say.' When Zac looked down at it he gasped to see his father looking back at him. Ramón stood next to him, Ed flanking the other side – and there *he* was, standing by the sheep wagon, looking typically petulant.

Zac smiled bitterly. 'This was taken before we left town on the fateful drive. . . .' He shook his head, muttering to himself. 'I don't even have an image of you, Pa.' Zac wiped a hand across his eyes. 'Would-be mayor of Dead Beeve Creek or not, we're gonna make that evil bastard Bryant pay for what he's done to us!'

Nestor nodded, and for the first time Zac noticed that he *did* resemble Ramón for a brief moment. Nestor stood and laughed loudly, embracing Zac, kissing him on the cheeks. '*Muy bien! Muy bien!* Now it is time for the vengeance of an *hombre*!'

Zac patted him on the back; somehow his grief was easier to bear now that somebody else shared his terrible load. Zac brought out some food and drink to Nestor in the bunkhouse. He made another brief appearance before retiring, and said he would speak to Tom in the morning. Zac dreaded telling his good friend the decision he had made.


'Are you sure about this, Jed?' Tom said as Zac stood saddling his roan. His older mount, Snowy the black gelding, was not up to prolonged cross-country travel at speed.

At last Zac turned and told his old friend everything. Everything he had not dared think about for the past seven years. 'I ain't sure about anything any more, Tom,' Zac said at last.

It was a long time before Tom spoke. 'We both know Bryant's a dangerous man, Jed. He's angry as hell that he never got to kill you!'

Zac nodded as he placed his loaded Remington into its saddle scabbard.

'What can you and a mangy little Mexican boy do against his might?'

Zac ignored the question, for deep down he knew Tom was probably right, but he had to do this, it was only right. Even if it meant getting killed. Now he realized that life lived without honour was no existence at all. 'If anyone comes snooping around here, Tom, you know nothin'.'

Tom nodded. 'Naturally.'

Zac swung into the saddle, put his hand out to his friend and shook it hard.

'When I get back, I'll get to breaking those fine colt mustangs I caught today. They've got my name on 'em!'

Pete Wilson, one of the foremen on the eastbound cattle cars loading up in Dead Beeve Creek, was supervising the cleaning of the cars before the next shipment. He took a long drag on his smoke and rubbed a hand over his stiff neck. It had been hot work over the past few days. Right now all he could think about was a cool beer in a shady saloon. When a shadow walked into his light, coming towards him, he held a hand to his eyes to see who it was. A smartly dressed man with impeccably kept sideburns and sober expression asked curtly, 'Peter Calvin Wilson?'

Wilson, a little taken aback, stood up straight. 'Who might you be, mister?'

'Elias J. Richmond, assistant to the director of W&E cattle transportation company.'

Wilson slowly nodded. 'And him?' Wilson motioned towards Richardson's equally sour-looking silent companion. He was a somewhat younger model of Mr Richardson, but just as stiff-necked, just as opinionated.

'My assistant, Mr O'Brien.'

'An assistant to an assistant!' Wilson remarked drily. He tried to muster a smile but could not. 'Well, gentlemen, as you can see, we're busy here. What can I do for you, Mr Richmond?'

Richmond, evidently feeling uncomfortable in a real working environment, moved uneasily from foot to foot. His usually pallid office-bound skin was showing the effects of too much sun, his nose wrinkled from the stench of cattle. 'Is there somewhere we can go to have some privacy, Mr Wilson?'

'Afraid I ain't got time for that, Mr Richmond. Say what you came here to say.'

Richmond and O'Brien exchanged glances. Richmond adjusted his expensive-looking silk neckerchief. 'Very well, Mr Wilson. If you want to have it out here in the open, have it, then! It has come to the company's attention that some stock has been going missing.'

Wilson furrowed his brow. 'Stock?'

'I believe that is the correct term for it. According to the 1886 inventory of supplies and stock, a black gelding was on a stock car bound for Silver Rock. Under your management, the animal simply seemed to disappear.'

'What?' Wilson choked, taking a step back from the two men as if they had suddenly become venomous snakes. 'I don't know what you're talkin' about! 1886? That's seven years ago!'

'It's all down here in black and white, Mr Wilson. Our new president Mr Dale Bryant has insisted we start looking at ways of minimizing loss through mismanagement . . . or theft.'

'Bryant!' Wilson reacted as if he had swallowed a whole chilli, choking to get the name out of his mouth. 'You ain't got no proof! Could've been anyone of those men on that car!'

'Can you prove it?' O'Brien piped up and was answered by a hard punch that sent his spectacles flying off his nose.

'I ain't gotta prove nothin', you goddamned little cuss!'

Suddenly there were rough hands on Wilson's

shoulders, dragging him backwards down the steps of the platform. 'You can't do this! I've got three thousand head ready to be shipped!' Wilson fought against Richmond's thugs, but it was of little use. Some of Wilson's cowhands ran over and tried to intervene, but were warned off by a gunshot from one Richardson's burly helpers.

'Maybe Mr Wilson will see sense from the inside of the jailhouse,' said Mr Richmond as he carefully descended the steps, a smug smile on his pursed lips. Wilson smiled too when he saw that Richmond's smart black suit was splattered with wet manure. Even more satisfying was the sight of O'Brien walking along with his spectacles perched back on his nose, except that now they were broken and askew.

*Idiots*, Wilson thought, then turned his mind to what might await him at the sheriff's office.

# CHAPTER EIGHT

The nightmares about his father dying, which had been absent for so long, now became a nightly occurrence the closer they came to Wyoming and Dead Beeve Creek. In one, Zac could hear his father's pitiful cries for help. It was so real that Zac woke up to find his cheeks wet where he had been weeping in his sleep. Nestor seemed troubled too, and was often up well before daybreak, as if he was too afraid to sleep.

Sometimes when he was quiet and alone Zac thought he heard his father's voice call him.

*Jesus Christ*, he thought, *I'll be glad when this is finished. One way or the other.*

When Zac had finished his meagre breakfast Nestor took a bottle out of his saddle-bag and handed it to him. 'You like, *si?*' Zac pulled a face uncertainly before taking a large swig from the bottle. He shook his head and gasped. Nestor, observing his reaction, laughed heartily at him. 'It is good, no?'

'No!' Zac wheezed, tears welling up in his eyes. 'Even for a seasoned drinker like me that is *fuerte*, amigo!'

'Finest tequila in Mexico, *compadre*! Not that watery horse piss you gringos drink!'

Zac shook his head again as he looked across the same landscape he had known seven years earlier, but under very different circumstances. Now they had dismounted and sat resting after days on the trail, Zac looked across at the town of Dead Beeve Creek. He had only visited the town briefly with his father, and Dead Beeve Creek had expanded since then. Now there were several more saloons along Main Street, a new mercantile, a telegraph office, even a bank. Like or not, it appeared that Bryant's wealth had made something of this town. *Yeah*, Zac thought, *using blood-money to buy it*. An uneasy feeling tied itself into a knot in his stomach. The tequila hadn't managed to give him much Dutch courage. He was not afraid, but was afraid of revealing his identity too soon, thus blowing his cover. He had come here to even the score. Bryant had to die. Still he hesitated. A sudden lack of confidence overcame him as he shot the young Mexican a glance. How did he know Nestor hadn't been working for Bryant all along? What proof did he have? A tatty old photograph? The fact that he called him *Zachito*, like his father used to?

'Why do we have to go into town right now, Nestor? *Por qué?*'

Nestor heard the hard edge to Zac's tone. His smile disappeared, a flash of anger sparked in his eyes. 'I know what you are thinking, Zachito. Now that I have lured you here, I will hand you over to those wolves!' He stood, his face inches away from Zac's as his voice became louder. 'I swear on my father's name, I am your *true* friend. As my father was to yours. We are here to buy ammunition, *amigo*, and all the supplies we can carry back to the widow's place. Once we get there we might be holed up for weeks! Together we must all find a way of getting rid of that murdering *cabrón* Bryant!' Furiously Nestor tightened his horse's cinch and mounted up. Zac felt guilty for ever doubting him.

'*Compadre,*' Zac said, putting a hand out to him, but Nestor ignored it, put spur to flesh and headed for Dead Beeve Creek at a gallop. 'By God, you're as fiery as your liquor, *amigo!*' Zac muttered under his breath.

By the time Zac caught up, Nestor was already heading into the gunsmith's to buy ammunition. 'I'll see you in a while,' Zac said briefly before Nestor went in.

He had forgotten to mention to Nestor not to call him *Zachito* in public. Someone would probably understand Mexican, and his identity would be revealed. For all his unrecognizable appearance, Zac still looked around a little self-consciously. His shoulder-length hair and beard marked him out from every man he could see around town. Not wanting to remain standing on display on the boardwalk, he stepped into Hickey's mercantile. He stood a while staring blankly at the commodes, having no idea what Nestor had planned on his supply list from this place. Aware that he was attracting glances from other customers, he moved on to staring at the horse blankets, wondering what was taking Nestor so long, Zac was vaguely wondering whether he could afford a new blanket when he heard raised voices coming from outside the mercantile. His instincts told him to stay inside, out of sight, out of trouble. But when he heard the high voice of a distressed female he had to act. When he got outside he saw a young woman, dressed in an expensive-looking fitted vest and white blouse, looking at her scattered boxes on the boardwalk, the floor strewn with tissue paper and lady's undergarments.

'You should look where you're walking, Miss High and Mighty! You don't own the boardwalk!' a scruffily dressed cowpoke with no front teeth yelled at her. He plucked from the floor one of her new purchases, a pair of pink bloomers, on the end of his boot and lifted it up for all to see. The girl flushed red at the humiliation of it. Then she rushed at him, pounding at him with small fists. 'Put that down at once!'

There was a small crowd gathering, and Zac was angered when he saw not one person intervene and help the girl. Some were even openly sniggering at her plight. All Zac's instincts told him not to get involved, but he couldn't just turn a blind eye.

'Do as the young lady says!' Zac demanded, releasing the catch on his Colt. By the way the cowpoke moved, Zac could tell he was drunk, and that made him twice as dangerous.

The cowpoke straightened up, fumbling for his six-shooter. 'This ain't nothin' to do with you, mountain man! Get out of here and go and kill a grizzly!' With that, the cowpoke trod on the pink garment on the boardwalk and ground it in with his foot. When he looked up, guffawing, he was met with the might of Zac's punch square on the chin. In shock, he tripped over his own feet and sprawled over the boardwalk. An equally drunken cowpoke came running to his aid. 'Jess, get up, you stupid ox! We gotta get outta here! Don't you know who she is?'

As he watched them disappear down Main Street, Zac blew out a sigh of relief that the law hadn't been summoned. Out of courtesy he reached down and collected up the young woman's fallen boxes. They were dainty, expensive looking things, some with pink candy-stripes, some with blue. All Zac could see was his dirty hands picking them up. He was glad he wore a full beard to hide his embarrassment at dropping the trampled pink bloomers back in the box. He'd never handled a *lady's* underwear before.

'Here you go, miss,' he said, at last looking directly at her. She was staring straight back at him so closely it was if her gaze was boring straight into his soul. She wasn't conventionally beautiful, her teeth were a little too large, her hair was a plain brown, the shape of her face and figure were full enough to indicate that she had never done a day's toil in her life. But Zac was transfixed. Her eyes, almost yellow-green, like a cat's, looked deep into his own. Zac double-blinked and looked away, uncomfortable. *Lord, where in the hell is that Mexican when I need him?* He wondered as he took a step back.

'Thank you very much, mister. I'm obliged to you!' the young woman said in a well-spoken voice.

Zac looked round. 'I reckon you won't have any trouble off that drunken bum any more, miss. Uh . . .' he hesitated when she made no attempt to carry on walking, 'do you need some help to find your escort?'

She let out a deep laugh. 'Escort?'

Dammit! She was not making this easy! He didn't

want conversation, he wanted to find Nestor, and get the hell out of there!

'Begging your pardon, miss, but I thought a young lady might need an escort around here.'

'I'm not that young! I am eighteen, you know!' She leant forwards to him as if telling him a secret. 'But you're right, I do have an escort, Mr Harris. I said he must stay in the buckboard, as my shopping today was of a *personal* nature.' She laughed again; it bubbled up in her throat, rich and infectious. 'How did I know half of town was going to be shown my undergarments on the end of that brute's boot!' She put out one of her lace gloved hands to him. 'I'm Olivia-Jolene. Most people call me Livvy-Jo. Less stuffy!'

Her handshake was firm, and Zac stumbled over his words. 'I'm, uh . . .' he just stopped giving his real name, 'Jedediah Johnson.'

'Pleased to meet you, "Uh" Jedediah Johnson! Now you must allow me to offer you some refreshment, by way of showing gratitude for standing up to that frightful brute. There is a good place that serves teas and pastries not far from here.'

Zac pulled away, as if she had just asked him to wear nothing but his holster in the street whilst reciting some Whitman and doing an energetic jig.

'Uh, no thank you, miss.'

A shadow crossed her face. 'Don't you drink tea?'

Zac smiled. 'Don't reckon I belong amongst all that fine bone china and extended pinkies! I'd probably just end up breaking something!'

She looked him up and down. 'You look fine to me.' Tension grew as Zac suddenly wondered how it would feel to kiss those full lips of hers. Livvy-Jo suddenly picked up the boxes, realizing they had been standing outside the saloon for a long time.

'You're probably right, Mr Johnson. No disrespect, but you look like you could do with a good feed, and I know the owner of the best eating-house in town.'

Zac held back and looked up the boardwalk towards the gunsmith's. There was still no sign of Nestor. Besides, he knew Nestor still had more errands to run. It would be bad manners not to accept an invitation from such a charming companion. He would be back before Nestor realized he was missing.

Chris Harris, ex-foreman of the Triple X ranch, sat by the livery in the buckboard as instructed by Livvy-Jo Bryant. He knew there would be hell to pay if his boss found out she was walking in town unescorted, but he figured she had a right to some privacy! Things had gotten worse for him at the Triple X since that time Reeve had tried to kidnap Livvy-Jo to make a point to the tyrannical Bryant. Harris openly wept when they caught Reeve, dragged him behind a horse around the ranch and then hanged him from a tree as a warning to others. Harris had been seriously disabled in a round-up one year when the steers stampeded and knocked him from his horse. Now he was a virtual prisoner, as if he *belonged* to Bryant. Harris had been assigned to watch over Livvy-Jo since her return from the ladies' college in the East. Harris was the longest-serving worker at the Triple X, and Livvy-Jo told her father he was one she felt most comfortable with as a chaperone.

*Yes,* Harris thought drily, *only because she knows she can sweet-talk me into allowing her to do exactly as she wants.* Besides, he could see her clearly from his vantage point here. Harris had watched Livvy-Jo grow up over the years and had seen her blossom into an intelligent and sensitive young lady. Harris smiled to himself when he thought these were qualities he had known in her sweet, late mother. Bryant didn't deserve such a wonderful person in his life. Harris left his post briefly to unhitch the horses from the buckboard and move them into the shade to drink. When he next looked up to see Livvy-Jo, she was talking to a stranger. Harris narrowed his eyes. Who the hell was he? He was helping her pick up her fallen boxes from the boardwalk. What had happened? Something must have occurred whilst he was busy out of sight with the horses. He had seen the stranger ride in earlier and hitch his roan to the hitching rail behind the gunsmith's shop, as if he didn't want it to be noticed. Harris calmly crossed Main Street to give the roan a surreptitious look. Its brand wasn't a local one. He had noticed the stranger wander into the mercantile as if lost, then, the next time he looked up, there he was speaking with Livvy-Jo. Harris didn't like it, he was *different*. He almost brought a smile to Harris's face as he looked at him, his long, thick, dark hair glowing in the sunlight. Jesus Christ, did he reckon he was Wild Bill Hickok with those glorious locks? Then, as the stranger and Livvy-Jo continued walking down the boardwalk together, Harris, slow as his mind was to work sometimes, suddenly realized who the stranger was.

# CHAPTER NINE

When a sheepish Zac returned to the hitching rail to collect his roan he was shocked to see that it had disappeared. 'Oh hell,' he whispered. He looked in at the gunsmith's but of course Nestor was long gone. Zac reckoned he must be as mad as hell. He stood a moment, wondering what to do next, when a tug came on his sleeve. 'Mr Zachito?' the young boy asked uncertainly. Zac gave a nod. 'I was told to tell you that your roan is over at the livery.'

Zac flipped the boy a coin in thanks. 'Oh, and the man said you're . . .' the boy paused with glee and let out a snigger, 'A goddamned gringo who'd better move your scrawny *culo* and ride like fury to catch me up!' The boy ran off laughing at being allowed to cuss with no recriminations. Zac rolled his eyes before riding on out of town. As he headed towards the White ranch, somehow everything felt different, looked different. The sagebrush that was trampled under hoof smelt beautiful, the breeze from the distant mountains was refreshing. He had never met anyone like Livvy-Jo before. He couldn't wait to tell Nestor about her. As he approached the ranch his throat caught when he saw the fields covered with grazing sheep. The last time he had seen a sheep had been seven years ago, on that fateful night. The last sheep he had seen had been lying in the river, screaming in agony and slowly dying from their injuries. He was shaken back into reality when the pack of guard dogs approached him, as usual. One or two he recognized, but most he didn't. And, unlike the usual breed, these were big, fearsome looking beasts. Two Mexican cowpokes rode up, as if he was expected. '*Hola*, Señor Zachito! *Bienvenido!*'

You could see they were cousins of Nestor; as well as having the same blue-black hair, they possessed the same nervous energy. Being greeted like a prodigal son made Zac nervous: what were these people expecting of him? He felt sick at the thought of letting them all down . . . but just as sick at plotting a man's murder, even though the man in question deserved to die in the street like a dog. As he unsaddled the roan in the stables, Zac suddenly felt apprehensive at the thought of seeing the widow again. As his roan was turned out into the corral, Zac's face lit up when a chestnut gelding approached him. 'Bayou!' he shouted, overjoyed that the gelding still remembered him after all this time. Zac ran up to Bayou, laughing. 'So that foreman *did* keep his word and return you!' Despite the onlookers thinking him loco, Zac didn't care and embraced Bayou fiercely. Even he was surprised at his own reaction. Zac cleared his throat and composed himself. 'You ain't even mine!' He laughed softly.

'Hello, Zachariah. Mr Wilson the foreman was most obliging when returning Bayou. We have made a good friend in Mr Wilson,' came a familiar voice behind him. He spun around and saw Helen White standing there, hands gently clasped in front of her.

'Helen!' Zac rushed over to her and lifted her off the ground in an all-encircling embrace. 'Thank God! I knew I'd see you again!' she sobbed. Zac was surprised to find tears springing up in his own eyes. When he set her down they both observed one another.

*Jesus*, thought Zac, *the years haven't been kind to you, Helen.* Her once beautiful golden hair now was more grey than gold, her eyes pale and dull, every hardship and worry of the past seven years etched into the lines around her exhausted face.

'I'm sorry to bring you back here, but now that Bryant is running for mayor of Dead Beeve Creek, it is becoming evident that he is dispatching any outstanding "problems" from the past, one by one.

Reeve, one of his workers was murdered horrifically in broad daylight. I have told Nestor it is too dangerous for him to remain here, considering who he is, but he won't leave me to face Bryant alone.'

'Neither will I!' Zac suddenly felt a surge of fury that Bryant was responsible for her present state.

She smiled at him and held his hands in her own calloused ones. 'I almost didn't recognize you, Zachariah, with your beard and long hair.' She pulled a sorry face. 'What a pity to hide the handsome man you are underneath there. . . .'

'You know it's necessary, Helen. I'm "the one that got away", remember? 'Sides, ain't nothing handsome about my ears. I ain't seen myself without this fur for at least five years!'

'Five years!' Helen exclaimed. 'And you are still so young. . . .'

Zac was saddened by Helen's deep melancholy and was pleased when Nestor came bouncing over to them.

'*Excelente compadre! Muy bien!*' Nestor held Zac in a grip so tight he could barely breathe. He struggled free, perplexed. '*Qué?*'

'*What?!* You are . . .' Nestor thought for a moment. '*Cuál es la palabra?* A genius!'

Zac smiled. 'You've been drinking too much of your firewater again, *amigo*!'

'No! I am not a drinker like you! I understand

your plan to get to Bryant through his daughter!'

Zac's calm smile vanished, and his face darkened. 'What do you mean?'

Nestor's expression also changed when he saw that Zac genuinely had no idea what he was referring to. Now his approach softened a little. 'What I mean, *amigo*, is that the *señorita* you met in town this morning is Livvy-Jo Bryant . . . Dale Bryant's daughter!'

Zac backed away as if stung, then pushed Nestor hard in the chest. 'No!' he yelled. 'No! You're lying!' Now anger reared its head, Zac's lips thinned, his fists clenched.

'You can't stand for me to be happy, can you? You're a jealous, good for nothing stinking *diego*!' As Zac turned to storm away somebody caught his arm. When he spun round he saw Helen standing there, her face ashen. 'I'm sorry, Zachariah, but Nestor is telling the truth. Livvy-Jo is Dale Bryant's daughter, now back from school in the East.'

Zac shook his head and sank to the ground, as if somebody wearing iron boots had kicked him in the guts. He pounded his fists into the ground until they bled. 'And I said I would meet her in town tomorrow. What an idiot!' Zac choked, staring at the ground.

Nestor and his cousins quietly moved away, leaving only Helen with Zac.

'I'm sorry, Helen, I reckon I've ruined everything!

What if she realizes who I am? That bastard Bryant knows everything! And now I know she is Bryant's daughter, it makes killing him even harder.'

Helen said nothing but sat down on the ground next to him. This was a situation nobody could have predicted, least of all Zachariah.

Livvy-Jo Bryant climbed on to the buckboard, her face beaming. 'Thank you for allowing me to go into town unchaperoned, Mr Harris. You're a real friend!'

Harris smiled back at her kindly. 'I just hope your father doesn't hear of it from somebody in town or we'll both be for it.'

Livvy-Jo turned to him, her smile fading. 'I was shopping. What's to tell?'

Harris looked straight ahead over the horses' heads as he said: 'The bearded stranger you disappeared with to the café for one thing.' He turned to her with a put-out look. 'My head will roll if your pa comes to hear of it.'

In her joy at seizing an opportunity to mention the stranger, she blurted out the question: 'Who is he?'

An exasperated glance came from Harris. He wasn't going to make public his hunch. 'Was hoping you'd tell me.'

'He says his name is Jedediah Johnson. He didn't say where he's from, or where he lives.'

'That's common enough, miss, in a railroad town.

Mebbe he's just passing through.'

'I've never met anyone like him.' She caught Harris's incredulous look and frowned.

'I admit I don't know many young men. Father would never allow it, but it's just that Jed is so easy to talk to.'

Harris chewed on the end of his smoke, agitated. 'Just one thing, miss; don't mention any of this when you get back home.'

Livvy-Jo crossed her arms and sat silently until a small smile came to her lips. She was going to see Jedediah again, tomorrow morning, in fact! What harm could it do?

Zac couldn't face sleeping in the widow's house, or the bunkhouse with Nestor and the others, so he took his blankets to the stables. Somehow he found the company of equines relaxing. They didn't ask endless questions, for one thing. There was only the sounds of them shifting in their stalls, the occasional blowing of a nostril. As he lay down, he could hear outside the calling of lambs to their mothers. That sound brought back so many memories. Zac closed his eyes in the darkness, thinking over the events of the day. As he sighed he fell into a doze.

Zac woke with an almighty start that sent his heart pounding in his chest. It was still dark. The horses in the stable had started fidgeting and kicking the doors of their stalls.

Then it started, the thundering of hoofs and cries of sheep. 'What the hell!' For a moment Zac was too terrified to move. It was like *that* horrific night all over again.

Forcing himself to become alert he leapt up and lit a lamp. Outside weren't ghosts from the past but real flesh and blood steers running amongst the ewes in blind panic. Zac thought he saw a rider but the man quickly disappeared when he saw the lamp.

'Goddamned coward,' Zac cursed as he quickly saddled his roan. The sheep were visible in the darkness, their white coats reflecting what little moonlight there was.

Zac identified the lead steer and managed to turn it away from the sheep that had been corralled overnight. Letting his guard down momentarily, he didn't see the other steer that had been running alongside them. It bumped into Zac's horse like a locomotive. It all happened in a flash, Zac didn't even remember falling, he just remembered the impact as the black ground came up to meet him. Now he saw Helen riding out on Bayou, followed by Nestor and three others. Between them they managed to drive the steers back on to Bryant's land. Zac got to his feet, winded, but otherwise unhurt. His roan had bolted back to the stables in fright.

'They must've seen me back on your ranch, Helen.

Bryant must know it's me, and that's why they did this—'

'Nothing you've done, Zachariah. This happens frequently. Thank you, boys, come back to the house, for some coffee,' Helen shouted over her shoulder to the others.

As soon as it was light enough to do so, Zac examined the damage. His roan was still jittery but otherwise undamaged from last night's events. Zac's heart bled when he saw the pointless killing that had taken place. A dozen ewes and their lambs had been trampled by the steers. A stiff breeze blew, adding to the depressing feeling of desolation.

Zac checked the barbed wire fencing and saw it had been cut straight through where Zac had seen the rider last night.

'Bryant always does this every time we dare to leave part of the flock uncorralled overnight.'

Zac hadn't heard Helen ride up behind him. *Christ, you're getting lax, boy,* Zac thought, thankful she wasn't an enemy from the Triple X.

Helen's visage was drained, eyes red-rimmed, as if she had been crying. She looked smaller somehow, as if she'd been physically and mentally crushed.

'We should have corralled the whole flock,' she said when she saw the trampled ewes. Zac looked at her with a mixture of sorrow and determination. 'Mrs White, don't you *dare* blame yourself for this!

106

You have the right to do whatever you wish on your own land, Helen! Don't you dare blame yourself for this!'

She looked up, slightly shocked by his raised voice.

'What happened here last night has made my decision perfectly clear, Helen. I'm still going to meet Miss Bryant as planned this morning.'

She looked confused, but forced a weak smile. 'As you wish, Zachariah.'

'And I'm gonna find a way to rid us once and for all of that poisonous son of a bitch Dale Bryant!'

# CHAPTER TEN

Zac stood in the morning light, clean and tidy ready for his trip to meet Livvy-Jo in Dead Beeve Creek. He wore his best suit. It was a little unfashionable, but smart enough. As Zac led his saddled roan from the corral he saw Nestor galloping back to the farm at breakneck speed.

'Zachito! Señora White has been summoned to Dead Beeve Creek! She has ridden on already!' Nestor shouted urgently.

'What? Why?' Zac felt his pulse quicken at the new turn of events.

'A messenger from the sheriff's office in Dead Beeve said Pete Wilson had been arrested and was asking for help.'

Pete Wilson? Zac took a moment to recall him. Then he remembered the cattle-car foreman who had saved his skin.

'What help? If we can give it, *amigo*, he's got it!'

'Before she rode on the *señora* believed Bryant was behind this.'

Zac let out a long weary sigh. 'He's tryin' to dispatch us, one by one. Nobody wants a mayor with a whole graveyard in his closet! Sure as hell ain't got time for this,' Zac muttered. 'I have some pressing business in town, *compadre*. Maybe you and your cousins should keep a close eye on this place while we're gone.'

'*Sí.*' Nestor nodded vigorously. 'Bryant's losing control and he can't bear it. Keep the faith, our time for retribution is coming, *amigo*!'

Zac nodded and pushed the roan into a lope, his mind racing. Why was he going to town to see Livvy-Jo? Helen's presence at the sheriff's office was going to cause complications. How were they going to help Mr Wilson? What did Zac realistically hope to learn from Livvy-Jo Bryant? She had been away so long she was almost a stranger to her father, she could know little of his business. When Zac approached town he noticed that different coloured flags were hanging between the buildings. There were electoral posters plastered to the walls wherever space allowed, promoting the candidate running for mayor against Bryant, Ted Montgomery. Zac studied the black-and-white image for a moment. This man was white-haired with a strong jaw and deep set eyes. The eyes of a thinker, Zac thought with admiration. As he turned away a man walked right up behind Zac and started pasting another poster on top of Ted Montgomery.

'Hey! What're you doin' that for?' Zac snapped at the withered old man before he scuttled off to wherever it was he had emerged from. When Zac looked back at the replacement poster, he gasped. Dale Bryant stared straight back at him. When Zac glanced down the street he saw it was blanketed with images of Bryant's loathsome visage everywhere you looked. He ground his teeth in a silent rage.

'Hello, Mr Johnson.' The lady's voice came from behind him. Smiling, Zac turned around and found himself face to face with Livvy-Jo and, unexpectedly, her father.

Zac stepped back at the sight of the real life Dale Bryant. Bryant's smile spread, taking pleasure in having startled the younger man.

'You look like you've seen a ghost, Mr Johnson!' He chuckled.

Zac had never been this close to Bryant since that dreadful night of the brutal attack when Bryant had 'clipped' his ears. Now being in such close proximity to the murderer sickened him. Dale Bryant. The man who haunted his nightmares for the past seven years now stood in front of him. Dale Bryant, cattle baron who had swapped his corduroy pants for a gold pocket watch and expensive frock-coat, carrying the excessive weight that came with corruption and power. Zac took a deep breath, for everybody's plans to rid themselves of this man depended upon his reactions during the next few moments. Those moments had arrived sooner than he'd expected, but the time had come for the performance of his life. He was well aware of Bryant's 'helpers' milling about the street, now and then surreptitiously looking over at them.

'Oh no, sorry sir. I was just startled, is all.'

Bryant's smile vanished as he looked Zac up and down. 'Startle easy, do you? Well, Mr Johnson, it appears I am indebted to you.'

That took Zac off guard. 'Indebted?' he asked cautiously.

'For helping my daughter the other day when she had a problem with an insolent cowhand. These days we don't tolerate such behaviour.'

Relief washed over Zac. 'Oh! That was my pleasure, sir. Weren't right to treat the young lady like that.'

'Indeed. And what are you doing in Dead Beeve Creek, Mr Johnson?' Bryant's speech was more refined than Zac remembered. There was no hint of the cursing, rough language that had once spewed forth from his mouth. Zac swallowed, his mouth suddenly dry. 'Just passing through.'

Bryant nodded slowly, his unnerving gaze never leaving Zac, as if he was trying to stare right into his very soul. 'Just passing through. Have you been helping out over at the White ranch?' The question punched Zac in the chest, but he replied quickly, to avoid arousing any suspicion.

'I did pick up a little work over that way, sure,' Zac said, straining to appear nonchalant.

'Like woollies, do you?' Bryant probed closely, his gaze never leaving Zac's face for a second.

'No sir. Them's dirty useless critters. Cows are more my thing, but I was needed over there to do the jobs those damned diegos had botched. 'Sides, I needed more dough before moving on.'

There was a silence that seemed to go on for hours, as Zac waited to see whether Bryant had bought his story. At length Bryant said: 'Well, that's what I figured. I could see by your clothes you were a ranch worker – you're not dressed like a gentleman! You have a lean and hungry look.' Bryant laughed, noting Zac's uncertain expression. '*Julius Caesar*, Mr Johnson. Don't you know William Shakespeare?'

Zac shook his head. 'Never met Mr Shakespeare, sir.'

Bryant roared with laughter, clapping Zac on the shoulder. Zac's jaw clenched tight, fighting against his instinct to knock Bryant out cold. *Bide your time*, the voice in his head kept telling him.

'Daddy!' Both men turned at Livvy-Jo's displeased voice. She stood uncomfortably on the boardwalk, her cheeks flushed with embarrassment. She didn't need to say another word; her look told her father to back off and stop making a fool of Zac.

'The sun is too warm now and I wish to visit the café for some refreshment, Daddy. I have some novels I wish to give to Mr Johnson by way of thanking him for his gallant actions yesterday.'

By her expression it was clear she meant *without any more interruptions.* Bryant looked at Zac, then at his daughter. 'Very well, Livvy-Jo. I will fetch Harris to chaperone you.'

Livvy-Jo smiled sweetly. 'As you wish, Daddy.'

As they watched Bryant walk towards the mercantile to fetch Harris, Zac felt a tug on his hand. 'Come! Before they return!'

Against himself, Oh God *how* against himself, Zac held back, painfully aware that dozens of eyes were still scrutinizing their every move. He allowed her to put her arm through his, respectably, as he pulled her back into a slow stroll. As their path passed the sheriff's office, Zac prayed that they wouldn't run into Helen or, worse still, the sheriff.

'What's the matter, Jedediah?' Livvy-Jo hissed through clenched teeth. This meeting was obviously not going as she had planned.

'You never told me you were Dale Bryant's

113

daughter.' The words spilled out before he could stop them, bitter and accusatory. She stopped walking, stunned.

It took her a moment to find her voice. 'That's why that cowpuncher was treating me like that yesterday.'

Zac dared not face her, scared of what his face might tell her. They strolled on again, not looking at each other. It twisted Zac up inside like barbed wire. All he wanted was to look at her, into those eyes.

'I can't see you any more,' Zac said suddenly in a small, strained voice. Livvy-Jo abruptly stopped.

'What? What do you mean?' Her voice rose a pitch. 'Why? Because I'm Bryant's daughter? I don't understand!' Angrily she pulled her arm out of Zac's. 'I can't help who my father is! I know a lot of people around here detest him because he's running for office. They are all jealous because he has made something of himself! I'm not blind and I'm not stupid!'

'Nobody said you were,' Zac said weakly, unsure what to do next. This was getting messier and messier by the minute; she was drawing attention to them. Zac glanced round before pulling her into a dark corner. She half-tried to fight him but he held her wrists and kissed her. She shoved him away, studying him for a moment before returning, on her terms, for another embrace. This time it was Zac who broke off. 'I'm sorry.'

They walked back into the sunlight just as Bryant returned with Harris. Zac's eyes widened as Harris stood facing him. Zac knew Harris recognized him and thanked the Lord when the older man kept his characteristic blank expression and said nothing.

'One hour, Livvy-Jo,' said Bryant. He strode off without even saying farewell. Both Zac and Harris watched him as he promenaded down the board-walk. Livvy-Jo was quiet, visibly changed by what had just happened in the alleyway a few moments ago. The following hour was uncomfortable for both men, neither being at ease in close proximity to lace, bone china and elegant little pastries.

When their time was up and Livvy-Jo climbed on to the buckboard once more, Zac could see that not even being able to speak to him as she wished, because of Harris's presence, was frustrating her. She said a polite goodbye before Bryant returned and stood between them. 'You'll be gone by election day, Mr Johnson?' he asked.

Zac struggled hard to quash his hatred for the man. 'I dare say, sir.'

Bryant barked a laugh. 'I *do* say, Mr Johnson. Good day to you.'

In a brief moment when Bryant's back was turned as he climbed on to the buckboard, Harris slipped Zac a piece of paper before hurriedly boarding himself. Zac made sure he was out of view of watchful eyes when he opened it. In poor writing and block capitals it read:

WHY ARE YOU HERE ZACARIAH SMITH? DID I HELP YOU BEFORE SO YOU COULD COME BACK AND GET KILLED THIS TIME? DON'T RECKON BRYANT RECOGNIZES YOU. YOU GET THE HELL OUTTA HERE, WHITE RANCH SOON TO BE WIPED OUT RECKON THEM MESSICANS THERE SOME-THING TO DO WITH THAT ONE I DRAGGED FROM THE RIVER AND BURIED THAT NIGHT.

Zac stopped. The Mexican he buried? A bitter smile crossed his face. Had Harris buried Ramón and his father? A sad smile lifted his cheek slightly. He read on:

BRYANT IS WIPING HIS PAST CLEAN. THAT INCLUDES WILSON AND ME. REEVE GOT IT. WIDOW NOT AT SHERIF OFFICE AT ALL. ALL A PLOY TO GET HER AWAY. GET OUT WHILE YOU STILL CAN. IF BRYANT ELE-CETED WILSON TO DIE AS AN EXAMPLE TO HORSE THIEVES.

The next section was underlined:

AND FOOLING ABOUT WITH LIVVY JO
DOWN THE ALLEYWAY WAS THE DUMBIST
THING YOU EVER DONE BOY.

Zac punched the wall, needing the pain to remind
himself what a fool he'd been. Now he wasted no
time. As Zac kicked his roan into a fast lope out of
town he cursed himself. He had put seeing Livvy-Jo
before Helen – his purpose in being here – before
everything. As he rode on he became aware of being
followed. The rider was coming up fast behind him.
In his peripheral vision Zac could see that the man
behind him was alone and was not posing a threat.
Zac suddenly pulled the roan into a sliding stop, a
trick most cowponies excelled at.

This was an unexpected move and Zac's pursuer
didn't change gait: he galloped on past them. Zac
watched as the man turned his horse around, frustrated.

'Jedediah!' he yelled.

Zac took a moment to recognize the man. As the
rider drew closer Zac saw it was Tom, from the
Meyers ranch.

'Tom?' Zac tensed, not willing to trust anyone any
more. 'What are you doing here?'

'We have little time, Jed. We must get to widow
White's as quickly as possible. I'll explain as we ride.'

As they came closer to the widow's homestead, Zac

immediately sensed something wasn't right. Somehow the silence fell as if following the after-shock of violence. Zac had noticed this phenomenon before, and it chilled him to the bone. Then he noticed that they hadn't been greeted by the farm dogs and his heart thumped faster. It was almost too late when Zac noticed the corpse lying face down in the grass. He felt queasy: the roan had almost trodden on it. Then Zac was relieved to see that the man was a stranger to him. His blood soaked clothes showed he had died of gunshot wounds.

'Tread carefully, Tom.' Half the flock had been turned out to grass and seemed to be grazing without agitation. Even so, Zac didn't trust the reactions of sheep; in his experience they carried on oblivious to danger until it was halfway upon them. Zac was just wondering where Nestor and the others were when a shot shattered the silence. Zac's horse half-reared and threatened to bolt. Zac turned him into himself, pulling him round in a tight semicircle until he calmed down. The bullet had slapped the ground in front of Tom. Another came, again aimed at Tom. Both men wheeled their mounts around, both animals' mouths were clamped tight shut in fear; both threatening to bolt at any second.

'Goddamn you, show yourselves, you cowards!' Zac roared at the invisible marksman.

'Zachito?' came Nestor's voice. Zac pushed the

roan closer cautiously, fearful of being pulled into a trap. Zac replied in his poor Spanish. Again Zac scanned the field but saw no sign of Nestor. Then suddenly one of the sheep in the field stood up on its hind legs, then another, then another. . . .

'What the hell. . . ?' Tom gasped. Hidden inside a whole sheepskin stood Nestor. The other 'sheep' on two legs proved to be his cousin, similarly disguised. 'Damned diegos!' Tom laughed in admiration. Then growled: 'You almost shot me!'

'What's happened here, Nestor?' Zac asked. Nestor shrugged his woolly shoulders.

'Some of Bryant's men came as we expected.' He let out a short laugh. 'They were not expecting *us* to be here, *no, compadre?* They will not return while we remain! We laugh as they cannot see who is shooting them! The sheep! Men in sheep's clothing, no? We shoot six *hombres* before they can shoot us!'

Zac grimaced as he paid closer attention to the men's disguises – hollowed-out sheep cadavers, with their decomposing heads flopping about uselessly. Though he found it repellent, he had to admire the Mexicans' ingenuity. He'd never have dreamt of staking out a place from inside a dead sheep!

'Good work, *amigos*.' Zac nodded at them all; then his smile faded as he remembered something. 'Has Helen returned yet?'

'No, *compadre*. You did not see her in town?' Nestor

asked, his smile also fading.

Zac swallowed hard. 'No.' A small flutter of panic rose in his chest. Harris had been telling the truth. He stood for a moment, wondering what to do. He already knew what to do, but was momentarily afraid to do it. He turned to Tom. 'My God, I'm glad you're here, Tom. I think Bryant is keeping the widow against her will. I'll bet over at the Triple X. In the morning the election will take place. If Bryant wins, Wilson dies as an example to everyone. Murdered to silence him before he can tell the public the truth about Bryant.'

'I didn't have the chance to tell you before,' replied Tom. 'I kinda knew something was going to happen. Wilson got a message to me as soon as he was arrested, but then all communication ceased. That's when I rode on out here. Sheriff O'Toole in Athens is my uncle.'

'Your uncle? And you never told me?' Zac withdrew from Tom, all of a sudden becoming the suspicious man he had been when they'd first met.

Knowing Zac only too well, Tom trod carefully. 'Honestly, I hadn't thought to mention it, Jed. I never wanted to mention anything from the past around you. My uncle has been looking for a way to get rid of Bryant for years. When he met you, you made him realize that he had to get rid of Bryant once and for all. He'd seen others with various body parts mutilated in a similar way to you. . .' he self-consciously tailed off. 'He still needs to find a way of getting rid of Bryant.' Tom looked at Zac, as if knowing what he was thinking. 'Legally, that is.'

Without saying a word, Zac went into the livery and exchanged the tired roan for a fresh sorrel. 'Defend the place, Nestor. I'm going to find Helen. If any bastard gets in my way over there at the Triple X, I'll sort him out.' He shot Tom a defiant look. '*Legally* or not.'

# CHAPTER ELEVEN

When Helen White regained consciousness she pan-
icked: she didn't recognize her surroundings. The
room, the bed, the wall hangings were all strange to
her. When she looked at her arms they were covered
in fabric which was not that of her own dress. She
noticed that her nails were dirty and her body ached
all down the back. Then she slowly started to recall
what had happened. *Yes,* she thought, *I remember now. I
was riding into town when Bayou tripped and fell. Not sure
how, as the ground had looked safe to me.* But a foot must
have found a prairie-dog hole, she decided. She
understood that she had knocked herself unconscious
in the fall, but what had happened to her since? Why
was she wearing a different dress? She felt a hot flush
of shame when she thought of somebody undressing
her without her consent, at seeing her exposed body
whilst she lay unconscious. Suddenly she sat up, wide

awake. The farm! She had to get back! She went to the door and shook at the handle. The door was locked. She ran to the window, for a means to escape and to pinpoint exactly where she was being held. She caught her breath but was not really surprised to see that she was inside the Bryant's ostentatious residence on the Triple X spread. She tried to open the window, but that too was barred. 'Damn him,' Helen cursed under her breath. Now a new resolve surged up in her veins. Bryant wasn't going to win. He was not going to break her; he had almost succeeded over the years, with his bullying, but not any longer. *No more acting like a victim*, Helen affirmed to herself. She said it again as the door was unlocked and Bryant strutted into the room. He paused, looking at her up and down in the fine blue-silk dress.

'Never thought anyone could ever equal my late wife Tessie in that dress. Well, lady, you've proved me wrong.'

Helen remained silent, her taut expression said it all.

'I suppose you're wondering how you came to be here?' Bryant asked, his characteristic basilisk glare making Helen want to forget her brave affirmations, and crumble.

'No, Mr Bryant. It is obvious to me that my horse fell and you,' she swallowed hard, '*kindly* brought me here to recover.'

Any amiability he had shown now vanished. This was not the reaction Bryant was expecting. Even now she kept up the pretence of being civil towards him. The only way he knew to express his frustration was through violence. He hurled the chair aside that stood between him and the widow. She started, but bravely fought the impulse to flee. She stood her ground.

'I brought you here, Mrs White, to tell you what is going to happen tomorrow. How it's going to be around here from now on!' he shouted in her face. He grew furious when she recoiled from him, and he punched the pillow next to her. She gasped but still remained steadfast. 'When I become mayor of Dead Beeve Creek the first thing I will do will be to hang that foreman Pete Wilson in the public square, as a deterrent to any other horse-thieves in the vicinity.' Bryant studied Helen's face carefully as he gave her the news.

*Horse-thief!* Inside she was screaming but she knew she must remain calm if she was to get out of this confrontation unharmed.

'You are to blame for the man's troubles. You and he were getting too well acquainted for my liking. You *will* become my wife! I *will* own your land – and *you*—'

'Never!' Helen went to strike at Bryant but he caught her wrist and started to squeeze.

124

She grimaced at the pain but refused to cry out. Dammit, she would not give him the satisfaction. 'I don't understand you, Helen. I have everything. I have status, wealth, power. If you became my wife you would want for nothing, You wouldn't need to do menial farm work – men's work – any more. I would dress you in the finest silks money can buy. You are the luckiest woman in the world! Most women would kill to have such an opportunity!'

When he saw the horror in her eyes he grew angry again.

'Why have you never offered me a kind word? You fawn over that Wilson. He has nothing to offer you, no money, no standing. Just like your husband, in fact. I did you a favour by dispatching that no-hoper hanging round your neck. Don't look so surprised, Helen, you knew I was responsible, you just never could prove it. Yes, he did fall off his horse and hit his head on a rock. Yes, that was what killed him, but the horse didn't bolt by itself. . . .'

Although it was agony, Helen wrenched her wrist out of Bryant's vicelike grip. Bryant was laughing. 'Murderer!' Helen yelled, tears springing into her eyes.

'Strong words. The weak don't deserve to live, Helen. Look at your flock – which, by the way is being slaughtered as we speak – the weaklings you leave to the mercy of the coyotes. That's nature,

Helen, the strong and the weak. I knew Wilson would get a message to you when my good friend Sheriff Bose arrested him. It's taken me seven years to put everything into place to become mayor of this town and I'm not giving up what's mine!'

He suddenly put an arm around Helen's waist, pulling her closer. 'You owe me one night, Helen, just for not killing you!'

When he moved his hands to her breasts, this time she succeeded in striking him. Instantly she knew she'd made a mistake. A bad mistake. Like a man possessed he lunged at her, knocking over the table and causing the vase to crash to the floor.

'You cold, stuck-up little bitch! Don't treat me with your disdain! You've played coy long enough! If I can't have you nobody can!' He pinned her to the floor and suddenly she felt his heavy weight on top of her. She cried out. 'Oh God, no!' Her thoughts were spinning as she tried to block out what might be coming next. Then she thought she heard footsteps outside the door, and then a voice calling for Bryant. When loud rapid knocks came on the door Bryant cursed but got up. Helen almost cried with relief.

Without looking at her, Bryant pulled on his jacket. 'Stop snivelling, woman. We'll finish this later,' he said, still not looking at her as he slid out of the barely opened door, as if trying to conceal that she was in the room. As she heard his heavy footfalls

126

fade away she sat on her haunches and wept. She looked at her bruised wrists, angry red, turning to purple. She had never wished anyone dead before, but now she wished she could be the one to deal the final death blow to this monster.

Zac stood back into the shadows of the outbuilding at the Triple X and smiled.

'You know, Tom, you're pretty good at creating a diversion!' They both watched as Bryant was seen walking quickly out towards the fire in the hayloft, which Tom had started.

'Reckon I've got Nestor to thank for blowing away most of the roughnecks from this ranch,' Tom replied. It seemed that darkness had fallen over the ranch quickly but they could still see Bryant's silhouette against the orange flames. Zac's smile faded as he watched Bryant.

'Yeah,' he replied absently. 'You know, friend, I could just take aim, and . . .' Zac paused for effect, '*Bang!* End of that evil bastard. No more Bryant. End of my nightmares. It would be a service to the community. All it takes is the tightening of my finger on the trigger . . . and then happy ever after.'

Tom looked at Zac thoughtfully. 'Don't count on that, Jed. Not sure it works that way.'

Zac turned away, running a hand through his hair. 'No, I guess it don't. And I know he has to live so we can expose him as being the tyrant that some folks in Dead Beeve genuinely don't realize him to be. Or else, to those who don't know any better, he'll be some martyr in the conflict between sheepherders and cattlemen. 'Sides, he is Livvy-Jo's father. I would not do anything to hurt her.' Zac's thoughts started to turn to Livvy-Jo, and he pulled himself back. It was agony to know she was inside the building, but he couldn't risk seeing her. It could ruin everything. Zac glanced at Tom. 'Better make use of the time we've got, Tom. The idiots! We need to work fast before they get back. We must find Helen!'

'Whoa! Easy, cowboy. This is one time we can't go in with guns blazing. Cover me, and *I* will find her. You're getting to be known, and we're too close to failing.'

Grudgingly Zac saw the sense in this and nodded for Tom to carry on into the building while he stood watch.

Livvy-Jo watched the fire from her open bedroom window. She was a little alarmed by the shouting and excited movements of the men below. She wondered how on earth the fire had started. She was glad she had asked for Harris to stay behind to keep her company. He was sitting outside her door and his presence made her feel safe. In between the rise and fall of the men's yells, she thought she heard crying coming from the room two doors away from hers. Having visitors to the house was not uncommon, but this felt different. The sobs drifted through her opened window, a woman's cry.

It sounded so desperate that Livvy-Jo could bear it no longer. She had to help the poor creature, and she rushed to her door to alert Harris.

'Mr Harris!' she cried as she flung open the door, but the chair was empty and Harris was gone. As she wondered where he had disappeared to Livvy-Jo saw him at the end of the hallway. All of a sudden she felt nervous, tentatively she walked towards him, her heart in her throat. The crying was louder now. *What was the woman doing here?*

'Mr Harris?' Livvy-Jo asked hesitantly. 'What's going on?'

He glanced over his shoulder and tried to pull the door to. 'Go back to your room, miss. I'll take care of this.'

'Take care of what?' Livvy-Jo walked past Harris into the bedroom. Then she took a step back. She knew the woman sitting on the bed. 'Mrs White! Whatever has happened to you?' The widow's face was red and blotchy from crying hard, her normally well kept hair was dishevelled. Livvy-Jo's eyes hardened when she saw the dress she was wearing. She shot an accusatory look at Harris before glaring at Mrs White. 'Why are you wearing my mother's dress?'

Mrs White sat dumbly. 'I—' She started to weep again.

'Mrs White was just telling me that she had a fall whilst out riding today. Your father brought her back here.'

Something didn't seem right. 'And he left her here without telling us, without offering her supper? Why here? Why not her own home? And why wear mother's dress?'

'I don't know, Livvy,' Harris said, looking a little uncertain himself.

Livvy-Jo knew Harris was keeping something from her. 'When we were in town today I saw you writing a note to somebody.' Harris's jaw clenched, his Adam's apple bulging as he swallowed hard. That pleased her, for now she knew she was getting closer to the truth. 'Who were you writing to?' she persisted.

'Me,' came the voice from behind them, so close it made Livvy-Jo jump. She hadn't heard the man come up behind them. Harris narrowed his eyes. Livvy regarded the man. Although he wasn't a youngster, his plump face gave him the look of youth. 'I was expecting to meet Mrs White in Dead Beeve. I worried when she never arrived early this morning. My enquiries have led me here. Now, if I may, I will accompany Mrs White back to her ranch.'

'How did you get up here?' Harris's hand dropped to his holster. 'Who are you?'

The man gave an easy, warm laugh. 'Easy, friend. Everyone else seemed a little preoccupied outside. I am sorry I took a liberty in inviting myself in, it's just that time is at a premium at present. I'm the new foreman over at Mrs White's ranch. Caspar Jones of Signal.' When he stopped talking an awkward silence descended. It didn't escape Livvy-Jo's attention that Mrs White acted as if 'Caspar Jones' was a complete stranger to her as well. Livvy-Jo knew *she*'d never seen him around before. As if noticing her guarded expression, Caspar Jones turned to her. 'Pleased to make your acquaintance, miss. When he found out I was riding out over here, Jedediah Johnson asked me to send you his regards.'

Livvy-Jo felt a jolt of electricity at the name. She tried, but failed, to stifle a smile.

'Jedediah Johnson? Well, Mrs White, this certainly changes things,' Harris said, looking relieved. A glance passed between Harris and the widow, as if he was reassuring her to trust this 'Caspar Jones'.

'Thank you, kind neighbours, for showing Mrs White such Christian charity in her hour of need,' Caspar Jones said with an unconvincing flourish. Mrs White stared at the floor, avoiding looking at Harris and Livvy-Jo. Livvy-Jo reached out and took the widow's arm gently. The two females' eyes met, Livvy-Jo's yellow-green ones questioning Mrs White's grey. 'Will you be all right?' When she saw the distress in

Mrs White's eyes, Livvy-Jo felt embarrassed at her own behaviour. She knew she had behaved like a inconsiderate, spoiled child for so unkindly harassing Mrs White over her mother's dress. Livvy-Jo somehow knew that none of this had been of the widow's own making. She seemed as meek as one of her own flock of woollies. As Mrs White was led away by Caspar Jones, Livvy-Jo thought it was as if she couldn't leave fast enough. When they had disappeared down the darkened hallway, Livvy-Jo and Harris looked at each other. Neither one had tried to stop them leaving. 'What was that about, Mr Harris?'

Harris put a shaking hand to his temple. 'Not sure I want to know, miss. Best you don't mention this to your father.'

'Which part?'

Harris gazed at her with weary eyes. 'Any of it.'

But Livvy-Jo had no intention of letting this incident go. Livvy-Jo had seen fear present in her home like nothing she had ever seen before. It was as if it was a prelude to something worse to come.

Hiding in the shadows outside, Zac watched as the men at last got the fire under control. He noticed how ineffectual Bryant really was in a crisis. His idea of the best person to supervise the men seemed to be downright boorish and simple: whomever was flabbiest around the girth and shouted loudest fitted the job. And boy, did he fit it! Zac felt hollow victory when he heard Bryant yell and curse at the unexpected absence of his roughnecks.

He hated Bryant even more when he thought of the six men who lay dead in the grass back at the widow's ranch. Still, he thought sourly, they had chosen to work for Bryant. Even so, the poor fools hadn't deserved death, Zac reckoned.

'C'mon Tom,' he muttered under his breath; time was running by too quickly and there was still no sign of him. He'd already had to knock a worker unconscious when the man had unexpectedly returned to the house. He had made sure he wouldn't be found until all of this was over, tomorrow.

Zac froze and withdrew deeper into the shadows when he heard voices inside the hallway, heading in his direction. He strained to hear who the voices belonged to when he felt cold metal digging into his back.

'Don't turn around, Zachariah Smith.'

Zac recognized the voice. 'Harris?'

Zac turned to his left at the sound of the hammer being pulled back on a revolver. Tom was aiming directly at Harris's temple.

'Give it up, friend,' Tom said, now unsmiling. Harris's lips thinned in anger.

'You fools, I'm only drawing on you to cover myself in case we get spotted. I ain't gonna be much use to you dead.' He looked at Tom. 'And you, whoever you are, what was that act all about? "Thank you kind Christian neighbours" eyewash? Should've just mentioned you knew Zachariah here. Or Jedediah . . . or whatever damn fool name he's calling himself now.'

When Zac caught sight of the distraught Helen he lost control. 'I know what you told me about not taking the law into my own hands, Tom, but now that brute Bryant has gone too far!'

Helen started weeping again. 'He admitted murdering my poor Ned!' she cried 'Then he tried to force himself on me. What would I have done if you two hadn't come?'

'I would've shot him myself, my dear,' Harris said bluntly. 'But tonight is not the time. I will keep Bryant from growing too suspicious. He will wonder what became of those six new roughnecks he just hired.'

'Why are you helping us, Harris?' Zac asked, still uncomfortable with the deadly metal digging into his spine.

'Because with every fibre of my being, I *hate* Bryant. He has brought sorrow to every single one of us. He once murdered somebody very dear to me in cold blood. My friend Reeve also knew what Bryant was, as he was there that night when he killed them sheepherders. Bryant made sure he was taken care of. Since I had that accident on a round-up a few years ago, I've been disabled.' Unexpectedly he smiled. 'Who knows, perhaps I was waiting for you to return, Zachariah Smith. I couldn't do any of this without you and your friends. But now you must go and prepare for the morning. One word of warning: apart from the hired guns of Bryant there is young Livvy-Jo Bryant. She's a smart girl, and knows something is wrong. She is like a daughter to me, and I don't want any harm to come to her tomorrow if she persuades her father to let her attend the elections.'

Zac smiled. 'Oh, I reckon she will find her way there. You have my word, Mr Harris. I'd rather die than hurt her.'

'Hope it don't come to that, son,' Harris said. He watched in silence as Zac and the others mounted up.

# CHAPTER TWELVE

Foreman Pete Wilson watched the moon through the bars of his tiny jail cell. The moon illuminated the big tree that the townsfolk had allowed to grow in the middle of the town square. The hanging tree. No need for man-made scaffolding when this monster of a tree was just as effective. His muscles were stiff where the brutish Sheriff Bose had ordered Wilson to be beaten where nobody could see the bruises. Wilson reckoned he had a broken rib. His gutless attackers had enjoyed pulling the much bigger man down to his knees. Not one of them could have taken him on in a fair fight, with his hands unshackled. Now Wilson sat on his cot and put his head in his hands, utterly bereft. With nobody else to turn to, he was now at the end of his rope. Tom Meyers hadn't arrived, neither had Helen White come.

*

Returning to Helen's homestead last night had been upsetting. When she'd dismounted from Bayou she had rushed to Zac and held him hard, her deep sobs shaking her whole body. He stroked her hair, comforting her. At last, it seemed, Bryant had broken this courageous lady, and Zac wondered if it were possible to feel any more hatred against this abhorrent man. He was grateful that Nestor and the others had already buried the six roughnecks before Helen could see them. Zac was truly thankful for that, not wanting Helen to be any more distressed than she already was. As they sat in Helen's small home, they all expected some form of retribution from Bryant. Nobody settled all night long. But no retaliation came, and that made the group even more uneasy.

Zac had barely slept and was the first up, almost wanting to cheer after surviving the night. But the euphoria at being alive faded at the thought of the unwanted business of vengeance, and he sighed a little. Today was the day. Perhaps his last day on earth.

He watched the sunrise with appreciative eyes; everything looked more vibrant and beautiful than ever. Zac felt certain he had evaded the bullets for too long and now, after a good run, the odds were stacked against him. Now they probably stood in favour of death. Now was the last dance in this prolonged game of vengeance. From today Jedediah

Johnson would be no more.

From today Zachariah Smith would return from the wilderness. Zachariah Smith, son of a murdered sheepman, now hell-bent on revenge. After seven years in exile he would now reveal his true self to Bryant. He would make the people of Dead Beeve Creek realize that their would-be mayor was a murderer, a torturer and a rapist. He would face Bryant one last time until one or both men died. In his daydreams Zac saw the faces of his father, Ramón, his mother and, now, Livvy-Jo. The last hurt the most, knowing he could never see her ever again after today.

After drinking black coffee he started to turn back the clock seven years. First casualty was the facial hair. Zac was going to miss his beard. It was like his mask against the outside world. It took him a while to rid himself of many years' growth, for it was wiry and thick. When he next looked in the mirror he was a little taken aback. He hadn't seen his clean shaven face for years. He pushed at the face with long fingers, as if it belonged to someone else. Somebody a lot younger, almost a boy. The cheeks were weathered from years of hard work outside, but the bottom half of his face, where the beard had been, was pallid from lack of exposure to sunlight. His mouth was more down turned at the corners than he remembered. *No wonder*, he thought.

Next he engaged the help of Tom in cutting off the long locks. Zac felt nervous, as not many people had seen his mutilated ears. They were a constant reminder of that horrific night. Tom was one of the very few, which was why he gave him the job. When Tom had finished cutting, Zac shivered at the unfamiliar sensation of cold air around his neck. Both men looked at each other.

'Good God, you look like the young 'un you really are!' said Tom. 'You ready, Jed?'

'Hell, yes,' Zac replied. He turned to Helen, who was obviously going to need some time to get used to Zac's new appearance. He noticed her eyes flicker to the mutilated ears. 'I want you to stay here, Helen.'

She looked insulted. 'I can't believe you would say that to me after what happened yesterday. After everything that's been happening, I've just remembered poor Mr Wilson in that jailhouse! What are we to do?'

'Stay calm. You stay close to Tom.' Zac looked around. 'Where have those Mexicanos gone?'

Tom frowned. 'Come to think of it, I haven't seen them for hours. I didn't even see them leave.'

'Aw hell! No matter, no time for that. Reckon Bryant ain't got 'em, they're far too savvy for him.'

All three took a moment to look at each other, nobody wanting to mount up and face their destinies, all knowing they could not avoid it any longer.

They all embraced briefly before swinging round their mounts and mounting up. Unexpectedly Helen kicked up dust as she urged Bayou into a gallop. 'C'mon boys, let's end this sorrow once and for all!'

A smile crossed Zac's face and his expression softened with affection at the widow's indomitable spirit. Then he glanced over at Tom.

'Helen's back!' he whooped, charging after her.

Dead Beeve Creek was still when the three riders dismounted and hid their horses out of sight.

In the increasing light, Zac noticed that every poster displaying Bryant's visage had been pasted over. Zac's eyes narrowed. 'What the. . . ?' It took him a long moment to register what he was looking at. Himself. A fifteen-year-old self with 'AQUI' painted in red beneath the drawing. The next one he came across bore uncanny likenesses of his father and Ramón. The caption was: ASESINADO. '*Murdered*', Zac said to himself. He was surprised to hear his own rapid breathing. The next poster he came to was one of the long-forgotten Ed. Under his image was written; DESAPARECIDO. As Zac continued to look around town, he saw that some captions were in English, some in Spanish. *Nestor!* Zac said to himself. *You son of a gun! You've been busy!* He wondered how he had managed to replace all of the posters without getting caught. Then he wondered where Nestor and the others were holed up now. Zac turned to Tom, who had just returned from looking the jailhouse over. 'Bad news, Jed. Don't reckon we'll get Pete outta there. Not without getting him and us killed that is,' he hissed. 'We've come to this whole thing too late! Should've acted days ago!' Both men glowered at each other. Zac felt sick at the thought that Tom might be right, but he pushed this unhelpful thought away so that his mind could become focused.

'I knew it would be impossible to bust him out, Tom. Our time to strike will come later, *after* Bryant has won this rigged election. Then I will confront him in front of the whole town, and expose him for what he is!'

Tom shook his head, as if pained. His usually convivial temperament disappeared and he unexpectedly punched the wall. 'Jesus wept! I went along with you because I thought you had a plan. A real good plan. Now you spring this on me. No offence, Mrs White, I know it wasn't any of your making, but you were a distraction, one that cost us precious time. Now we get here with no men to fight with, our only ammunition is what we hold in our gunbelts. All we got is a man little more than a boy with big, noble ideas of vengeance but nothing to fight them through with!'

Zac felt himself starting to shake, partly through

anger, partly through anxiety. Oh God, this couldn't be happening. Not now he'd come so far.

Tom still hadn't finished venting his anger. Now he looked at Helen. 'I don't know if you realize the gravity of the situation, ma'am. Pete got pulled into this ugly mess because he's a just and good man. Now because of what he knows, he's gonna hang for it! And you. . . .' he spun back round to face Zac, testingly close, 'I told you them damned diegos ain't never no good, but you wouldn't listen. You rode off with that Nestor because he happened to have a photograph of you and your dead pa. That's what you base your trust on? Now, all those cowardly *amigos* have done for you is deface some posters and then vanish, leaving you high and—'

Tom never finished the sentence. The blow to the back of his head came from behind, and he stumbled before falling into the garbage by the side of the alleyway.

Zac had already unleathered his Colt and Tom's attacker emerged from the shadows.

'*Yo soy Nestor!*' he said to the unconscious Tom. '*No diego!*'

Although it shouldn't really be amusing, both Zac and Helen tittered. Then Zac rolled his eyes at Nestor. 'He's going to be like a bear with a sore head when he wakes up,' he told him as they both carried Tom away to conceal him somewhere where he wouldn't attract attention when he came round.

'Don't worry, Zachito. He hates me anyway!' Nestor growled.

'Hell, he's got reason to be sore at me,' Zac replied. 'If he dies, he'll leave his poor ma to run their ranch on her own.' He stopped when he saw Helen's indignant expression.

'Why not? You think she won't be able to, just because she's a woman?' She frowned.

'Let's say Mrs Meyers sure ain't you, Helen!' Zac glanced down at Tom. 'Shame Tom's out of action though, I needed another gun. We need to stake out the town square until this afternoon, when the results are announced. When Bryant sees those posters, he's gonna go wild. Even if he rolls into town later this morning, a hellava lot of voters will still have seen them already. Reckon the sheriff will set about removing them though. It's in his interest for Bryant to become mayor.' He looked at Nestor. 'How defended are we?'

'We already have many of us up there.' Nestor pointed up to the roofs.

'Good work, *compadre*.'

The trio withdrew as the townspeople were starting to wander out on to the boardwalks. Some stopped and looked at the posters. 'How did you manage paste up the posters without getting caught by the night watchmen?'

143

'Zachito, some men will listen only to this.' Nestor patted at the deadly metal in his holster and laughed. Stationed on their rooftop vantage point, they settled down, closely watching the activity down below in the streets. The longest wait of their lives had begun.

Old Harris had been on edge all morning, Livvy-Jo thought as he and her father silently readied themselves for their trip into Dead Beeve Creek. Bryant was uncharacteristically withdrawn, as if he had now put up an invisible wall between himself and everybody he encountered, including Livvy-Jo. He had forbidden her to accompany him and Harris into town for the election results and, surprisingly, she had accepted this with no protest. If she was honest, she was still shaken by what had happened last night with their neighbour Helen White. She hadn't mentioned it to her father, as it had been late when he eventually returned to the house, and he had been furious that the outbuilding had been damaged beyond repair.

Livvy-Jo had heard his violent rage downstairs, and for the first time in her life she was afraid of him. She reassured herself that Harris was still around, but she missed her mother terribly, desperately. She was sure this wouldn't be happening if she was still alive. Suddenly, somehow, she knew, she *knew* Helen

White's terror had been caused by her own father. And where did Jedediah Johnson, the object of her affections fit into all this? She waited for an hour for her father and Harris to ride on ahead in the buckboard, then she mounted up and followed them, unseen, into Dead Beeve Creek. If nobody was going to give her answers, she would find them out by herself.

Dead Beeve Creek was now a flurry of activity. Makeshift stalls were selling cooked food and refreshments, catering for folks relaxing into the carnival mood of the day. When Pete Wilson was led out from the jailhouse, he was met with jeers and missiles being thrown at him. He was dragged into the town square and forced up on to the makeshift platform by the side of the mighty hanging tree. He was flanked by a puffed-up Sheriff Bose, who grinned with satisfaction.

'The animals!' Helen cried in disgust when she heard an enterprising vendor selling beers, sarsaparilla and pretzels to the morbid townsmen loitering around by the hanging tree, hoping to see some macabre 'entertainment' later.

'Easy, Helen. Look! here comes Bryant at last! Why's he so late in getting here? Shouldn't he be stirring up the voters to give him their vote?' Zac sat back. 'Jeez, I forgot . . . his victory is certain! As far as

145

he's concerned, he's already won!' Zac watched as Bryant caught sight of one of the sheepherders' posters. Zac could tell even from this distance that his body stiffened in shock. Then his hangdog side-kick, Harris, stopped in his tracks directly behind him. Zac turned to Nestor and play punched him on the shoulder. 'You are a genius, *compadre*!'

The two men's attention was so fixed on watching the developments down below that neither one noticed Helen slip away.

Helen didn't know where she was going, but she knew she couldn't bear to be a spectator in what was quickly becoming a carnival. For God's sake, an innocent man was about to hang down there, and all anyone could think about was drinking cold beer and munching on liquorice sticks. As she climbed down her eyes adjusted to the gloom. She was star-tled when she saw a figure coming towards her on the stairs. As the figure drew closer, she dared to relax slightly, even though she knew she was a Bryant. Helen smiled at her warmly, then Livvy-Jo spoke.

'I need to hear the truth, Mrs White,' was the girl's sober greeting.

'Miss Bryant. . . .' Helen hadn't expected this, and she tried to think of an answer.

Coming towards her, Livvy-Jo Bryant aimed a pistol

she had been concealing under her skirt. Helen felt the all too familiar beginnings of dread when she saw how Livvy-Jo was unpredictable, tense. 'Messrs Smith & Wesson insist you tell me what you know! Tell me everything . . . now!'

Helen surprised them both when she smacked the weapon out of Livvy-Jo's hand with such angry force that the younger woman staggered back a couple of steps.

'You silly girl! Why did you come? You shouldn't be here!' Helen spat, but Livvy-Jo stubbornly stood her ground.

'I need to know the truth about my father, Mrs White. Over the past few days, I'm already seeing he's not the man I remember before I went away to school.'

Helen hoped Zac and Nestor hadn't heard the scuffle on the stairway. She looked at Livvy-Jo; for all her previous bravado, she now sat wide-eyed and vulnerable on a step. Helen released a sigh so long it was as if she was breathing out her very soul. 'You deserve the truth, Livvy-Jo, painful as it is for me to relate . . . but I must. As you wish, I will tell you everything. . . .'

Pete Wilson's death warrant was signed. As the results of the election came in, it was no surprise to learn that the winner was Dale Bryant. Dale Bryant, cattle baron, man of substance and proprietor of many of the businesses in town, was now the new mayor of Dead Beeve Creek. Many of the townsmen had been drinking for nigh on six hours and were now becoming a little rowdy. When one threw an egg and hit Bryant on his silk vest, his face turned almost purple in barely suppressed rage. Bryant pointed a finger at the wrongdoer; immediately the man was pushed to the floor by one of Bryant's heavies and was set upon by two other men.

'Thank you for giving me the opportunity of demonstrating just how quickly justice is now served in Dead Beeve Creek!'

The crowd grew silent, the festive atmosphere had suddenly become apprehensive.

'There will be law and order in this town from now on! Any breaches, no matter how petty will be subject to stiff punishment.'

The mood changed from macabre interest to horror when Pete Wilson, a sack over his head and his hands wrenched behind his back, was dragged on to a horse, a noose roughly pulled around his neck. With the noose still around his neck, in a last-ditch attempt to escape, Wilson clumsily managed to slip off the horse's back, but was dragged viciously back, now hollering in fear. Bryant now had the same expression that he'd had that night Jeremiah Smith was murdered. 'This man is a horse thief! My word is

now law around here, and I say we don't tolerate
thieving!'

All of Zac's new-found confidence evaporated at
this new turn of events. 'We gotta get down there,
Nestor!' he urged. Things weren't working out in the
way that, after years of imagining the scene, he had
thought to reintroduce himself to Bryant. But there
was no time to regret the present turn of events.
Wilson was sitting precariously on the horse. If the
animal bolted it would leave him to swing like a pen-
dulum. Zac gritted his teeth and tried to shoot the
rope that was slung over the tree. An impossible shot,
and of course he missed, but he succeeded in alerting everyone to their presence above. Zac and Nestor
threw themselves to the floor as bullets whizzed
above their heads, they were relieved to hear the
shots answered by their *compañeros* on the other roof
tops.

'We gotta get down there before this turns into a
bloodbath,' Zac said, slotting more bullets into his
gunbelt. As Zac emerged from the building he had
his .45 pointed straight in the direction of Bryant.
Zac braced himself for the inevitable hail of bullets to
strike his body, but they never came. Why wasn't
anyone shooting at him?

When he caught sight of Zac, Bryant took a step
backwards, as if Zac was a ghoul risen from the grave.
His eyes flickered up to a poster, then back at the

real, very much alive Zachariah Smith. A small gasp escaped his lips. 'What the hell?'

Leathering his Colt, Zac went over to Pete Wilson and steadied the horse. 'You OK, Mr Wilson?' Zac untied his wrists and Wilson lifted the noose back over his head. As Zac helped him off, he half-fell to the ground. Now Zac turned his gaze on Dale Bryant who stood stock still on the boardwalk, as if awaiting Zac's next move.

'I reckon you remember me now, Mr Bryant. I'm Zachariah Smith. Remember that night down at Dead Beeve Creek seven years ago when you did this to me?' Zac said, tugging at what remained of his butchered ear lobes. 'You disfigured me, killed my dogs and flock and' – Zac walked forward, unblinking – 'you murdered my father and his fellow sheepherder in cold blood.'

Bryant looked at all the upturned faces of the townspeople, left to right, every person was watching his next move. Suddenly he let out an unnecessarily loud guffaw. 'Sheriff Bose! Get this deluded boy out of here! He doesn't know what he's saying!'

As the sheriff started to walk towards them, the sound of gunfire burst in the air. The crowd parted as Sheriff O'Toole from Athens rode into the square, followed by his nephew, the now conscious Tom. 'Let Mr Smith speak, Bryant,' the old sheriff commanded. Defiant, Bryant crossed his arms. 'This little turd's got nothing on me! Aw, was I supposed to have killed his sheepherder daddy and some thieving diego?'

Nobody saw the knife coming until it found its target in Bryant's leg. 'No *diego!*' cried Nestor as he ran at Bryant. 'My father was no thief! Do not dare dishonour the name of Ramón Jesús Hernandez! *Asesino!* Murderer!'

As he crashed into Bryant, Nestor was blocked by a huge palm over his face, a debilitating punch in the guts and his own knife being thrust into his side. Bryant flung him into the crowd like a rag doll. Unfortunately the wound to Bryant's thigh was merely superficial. He looked around, slightly alarmed that nobody was coming to his aid. He smoothed out his waxed moustache haughtily and he pig-headedily carried on his charade of supremacy. 'Accusing a government official of such a heinous crime is against the law! And intentionally wounding one is a hanging offence!' Zac looked with concern at Nestor, his stab at revenge had ended in him being stabbed. He was being kindly attended to by some outraged members of the crowd.

Bryant's stare returned to Zac. 'Your little Mexican boy has more guts than you and your father put together. Give this up, boy. There is only your incon-sequential word against mine. Don't you know who I am? I have the best lawyers anywhere! You have no proof! Besides you, there are no other witnesses!'

'Oh, but there are,' Sheriff O'Toole replied. Nobody had taken any notice of the blond-haired man who had ridden alongside him into town. 'Meet Edward Lampert, former herder with the Smith sheep outfit. Witness to the illegal slaughter of stock, criminal damage to sheep wagons and to the brutal murders of Jeremiah Smith and Ramón Jesús Hernandez.'

Zac caught his breath. It was Ed! The Disappeared One! Where had he been all this time?

'He is willing to testify against you in a court of law,' O'Toole continued in his sober drawl. For all his arrogance, it was clear to everyone that Bryant was becoming worried now. In his fear he lashed out at O'Toole. 'You senile old son-of-a-bitch! He's just some bum you've picked up off the streets!'

'No, Mr Bryant. Both Mr Lampert and your worker Mr Harris buried the bodies of the murdered men. I met young Mr Smith in Athens immediately after your savage attack upon him. Although I took an educated guess that you were the perpetrator, Mr Smith fled before I had time to question him. I had no viable evidence against you . . . until now. The tenderfoot candidate for mayor, Ted Montgomery, was actually put up by me. I knew how much you wanted control of Dead Beeve at any cost.'

Bryant had become calm as he turned to Harris. 'You weren't never any good, Harris!'

152

Nobody could stop Bryant as he went for his .45 and shot twice at Harris, who was standing by the buckboard behind him. In a futile attempt to defend him, Zac let off a shot, finding a target in the right hand side of Bryant's torso. Now no longer concerned about retribution, Zac ran to Harris. He was on his back in the dirt, dark blood rapidly creating a disturbing circle around him. Overcome, Zac fell to his knees, and grasped Harris's hand. Two bullets had entered his body, one in the lower abdomen, one near his heart. Suddenly Helen appeared by his side with a distraught Livvy-Jo. With noticeable effort, Harris spoke, although it was barely a whisper. Sheriff O'Toole had dismounted and also stood at Harris's side. 'I'm goin' to hell, Sheriff,' Harris said choking as blood bubbled up in his throat. Silently a tear ran down Zac's cheek, and he squeezed the shot man's hand. 'No, Mr Harris, no. You're a good man, the best of men. You saved my life.'

'But I didn't stop Bryant taking your father's.' Harris turned his head to one side and became still. Livvy-Jo now grabbed his other hand. 'Please don't go!' She started to cry. 'Don't leave me.'

Zac squeezed Harris's hand harder as he felt him fading. He willed him to live. What would they all do without his constant benevolent presence in the background? Zac was surprised at the overwhelming emotion surging up in his throat, and he could barely speak. 'Now you'll get to have that drink with Reeve, *friend*,' he whispered.

He stood up. Wiping a hand across his eyes, Zac threw his jerkin on the floor as he strode towards Bryant. The exchange happened faster than anyone could have anticipated. No words, no rules, just basic survival. The fastest draw and the dead. Zac hit the ground first as the bullet in his chest propelled him backwards. He hit the ground hard and was paralysed with shock.

It was then that Livvy-Jo lifted her pistol at her own father.

Bryant laughed in her face. 'I ought to kill you, *murderer*,' she hissed. 'You're not my father any more.'

'And where did you get the money to buy all your dainty things, *girl?*' Bryant snarled. The pain from the bullet in his leg caused him to bellow out in agony before crashing to the floor. A breathless Zac staggered over to Bryant and put a boot on his wrist to halt any twitchy fingers looking to return fire. 'I ain't gonna kill you,' he wheezed, now barely able to focus. 'I've seen enough bloodshed to last me ten lifetimes. No, I'm gonna do something far worse.' Their eyes met. Resolute brown meeting Bryant's cold blue. 'I'm gonna marry your daughter!' Zac stared into Bryant's eyes before he surrendered to the pain and lay down on the ground. He could feel his blood seeping into the ground around him. But strangely enough, that was all right. He was at peace now. He had done it. It was over.

# CHAPTER THIRTEEN

Zachariah Smith had been dreaming. At least, he thought it was a dream, for it had been so lucid he wasn't sure. In it he had seen his father and mother again, both free of illness and injury. But the pull of the surrounding voices was stronger and brought him back to consciousness.

'*Hola* Zachito! See! I told you he would not die!' Zac blinked at the jubilant Nestor, then smiled.

'*Hola, compadre!* Thank God! I feared you were dead!'

Nestor smiled broadly. 'It will take more than a letter opener in the side to kill me, *amigo*!'

Zac looked down at his body and saw his chest was bandaged up like an Egyptian mummy. Sunlight streamed through an unfamiliar doctor's window.

'Seems you just won't die!' came the mellow voice of Sheriff O'Toole. 'And thank the Lord for that! The bullet passed right through you, came out of your side!' Tom came over and shook Zac's hand, then embraced him round the shoulders. 'Don't forget when you're fit, and out of the doc's, you have those mustangs to be broke, Jed.'

Zac nodded. Helen came over and kissed him on the cheek. 'Thank you,' she whispered.

Although it hurt like hell, Zac put an arm up around her, breathing in her sweet smell. He thanked God she had made it through the horrendous nightmare. His breath caught when Pete Wilson hobbled forward. Neither man spoke, but the eyes said a mutual understanding of thanks.

'What became of Bryant?' Zac asked suddenly, as if just remembering.

Everyone exchanged glances. 'In the end the townsfolk meted out their own justice. Bryant took the place on the end of a hang rope instead of me,' Pete Wilson said with little joy in his voice.

'The folks of Dead Beeve Creek sure got their money's worth,' Helen said, shaking her head in disgust. 'The sick bunch.'

'That Sheriff Bose hot-footed it out of town before anyone could make him answer for his part in all of this,' O'Toole added. 'We'll find him, though. The cowardly bastard.'

The pain and the newly divulged information made Zac feel queasy. Then he remembered Harris. Zac licked his dry lips, almost afraid to ask the question. 'And where is Livvy-Jo?' Zac's heart pounded faster when nobody answered immediately. 'We're not sure ourselves, Zachariah,' Helen said at last. 'She seems to have holed herself up somewhere. Understandable, after what the poor girl has been through.'

Zac nodded as he closed his eyes. He welcomed sleep now. Everything was less complicated there.

They buried Harris next to Reeve's grave outside the Triple X. They all reckoned that was what he would have wanted.

Days passed and turned into weeks, and there was still no sign of Livvy-Jo. Ed had taken Zac and Nestor down to the place by the creek where he and Harris had buried their fathers. Ed was still the same, untalkative fella of seven years ago. When asked what had happened to him, he'd shrugged his shoulders. 'I thought you were dead, Zac. I cut outta here and never looked back. Only heard you were alive when I got work on a different drive.' Zac never asked any more after that.

As all three looked soberly at the wooden markers, both Ed and Nestor took their leave. Then they saw an ashen Livvy-Jo making her way towards Zac.

'Livvy-Jo!' he said 'Are you all right?'

'I was thinking about what you said,' was her greeting.

Zac rushed towards her as quickly as his pain would allow him to move. 'What did I say? I don't even listen to myself!'

'You said you wanted to marry me.' She said the words without smiling. 'Can you ever love somebody like me. After all *he* did to you?'

Zac pushed her hair back from her face. 'None of that was any of your making. I'm not sure I'm much of a catch. Can you love someone who has nothing to offer you?'

She smiled as she pulled him closer. 'I've been thinking about it and decided I've now got a ranch to run.' She paused. 'I'm gonna make you work hard, *cowboy.*'

Zac gave her a long smile. 'Cowboy? Naw, I was gonna work over at Helen's with Nestor, then return with Tom to the Meyers ranch. But really I'm a sheepherder through an' through, I reckon.'

She looked at him slyly before putting her arms around him. 'I guess there could be room on the Triple X for a flock, if that's what you want, *woollie*!'